A Season of Comebacks

A Season of Comebacks

KATHY MACKEL

G. P. Putnam's Sons   New York

G. P. Putnam's Sons, a division of The Putnam & Grosset Group,
200 Madison Avenue, New York, NY 10016.
G. P. Putnam's Sons, Reg. U. S. Pat. & Tm. Off.
Published simultaneously in Canada.
Printed in the United States of America.
Design by Patrick Collins.
Text set in Garamond Simoncini.

Library of Congress Cataloging-in-Publication Data

Mackel, Kathy.   A season of comebacks / Kathy Mackel.   p.   cm.
Summary: Ten-year-old Molly competes for the attention of her father, who seems to be
only interested in cultivating the talent of Molly's older sister, Allie, a star softball pitcher.
[1. Softball—Fiction. 2. Sibling rivalry—Fiction. 3. Sisters—Fiction. 4. Fathers
and daughters—Fiction.] I. Title
PZ7.M1965Se 1997   [Fic]—dc20   96-6882 CIP AC
ISBN 0-399-23026-2

10 9 8 7 6 5 4 3 2

To the TAP Fire

A Season of Comebacks

Chapter One

The world revolves around my sister, Allie.

Okay, maybe not the whole world. But our corner of it does. You see, Allie is *the* Allison Burrows, the best softball pitcher in the state of California. Anyone who knows anything about fast-pitch softball knows Allie.

Nobody knows me. I'm Molly Burrows, the ten-year-old shadow of the great Allie. I'm expected to worship my sister as much as the rest of her world does.

I refuse. I have better things to do with my life.

It wasn't always like this. For most of our lives, Allie and I got along pretty well—for sisters, that is. We played dolls and trucks and Monopoly. We rode our bikes and built tree forts and hung out with the neighborhood kids. We played softball and baseball and stickball. But around the time my sister was nine and I was seven, Allie stopped playing dolls and trucks and starting playing softball and more softball. She got tall, she got strong, and she learned to pitch a softball faster than anyone imagined a little girl could. Before we all knew it, Allie was attending clinics and working with a pitching tutor and talking to college coaches about the amazing future she had.

Nothing amazing happened to me. I stayed the same old Molly.

Last summer Allie took her first step to greatness when she and her fastball led the Brookdale Blazers to the State Championships. All of California watched as eleven-year-old Allie Burrows and her teammates swept away the big-city teams and captured the title.

Even before softball season started this spring, reporters buzzed around Allie like thirsty mosquitoes. The TV people filmed her pitching. They had a state trooper hold a radar gun on her, then he gave her a speeding ticket! Everyone thought it was cute. I thought it was sickening.

The whole world—okay, our corner of it—was predicting that this was the year. I mean big time—*the year!* My twelve-year-old sister was going to lead the Blazers all the way to the National Championship.

But it didn't work out that way. Starting with Opening Day in April, Allie's life was one disaster after another. Nothing worked out the way it was supposed to and there was nothing anybody could do about it. And I have to admit this—I found it interesting to watch Allie's life fall apart.

Until my life began to fall apart, too.

◆　◆　◆

The night before Opening Day, Dad sat at the kitchen table, putting together the Blazers' lineup. My father, Tom Burrows, is the coach of the Blazers and softball is his life. Before every game he does the same thing: writes, erases, thinks, checks statistics, writes again, erases again. Allie peered over his shoulder, making suggestions about who should bat where but "just make sure I bat cleanup."

Mom walked in with a load of laundry. As she dropped the basket on the counter, she may as well have dropped a bomb.

"Tom, you haven't forgotten that Allie's getting her braces tomorrow morning, have you?"

Dad looked at Mom like she had just grown a second head. "Cancel the appointment," he said, in the same tone of voice he uses when he tells us to clean our rooms. Nothing interferes with softball.

Except Mom isn't a kid and that tone of voice doesn't work with her.

"I made the appointment three months ago. I won't be able to get another one until September." Mom still believes there is life outside of softball.

"My mouth will hurt and I won't be able to pitch." That's Allie—she inherited the "softball is my life" stuff from Dad.

"Have someone else pitch," Mom reasoned.

Dad exploded. "No way! Channel 7's coming to see Allie pitch. And at least two papers are sending reporters. The more press coverage she gets, the better."

"For goodness sakes, Tom, the child is not running

for governor! And I'm sure Allison doesn't want to go on TV with crooked teeth."

"Oh, Mom," Allie whined, with the "Mo-o-o-o-m" lasting a record-breaking five seconds. "Come on, it's Opening Day." The "D-a-y" stretched three seconds and rattled my eardrums.

"Diane," Dad said.

"Tom," Mom said. "She's keeping the appointment."

My sister got her braces in the morning and was allowed to stay home from school to take aspirin, drink cold drinks, and rest for that evening's game. Dad took the afternoon off and by the time I got home from school, he and Allie had already gone to the field.

"What the heck are they doing at the field so early? The game's not for two hours," Chris said as he rummaged through my refrigerator, looking for his chocolate pudding. My mom always left chocolate pudding for Chris and tapioca for me for our after-school snack.

Christopher Reardon lived across the street and had been my best friend as long as either of us could remember. He was smart, funny, and good at sports. He was always in a happy mood, except when Allie was around. They used to be good friends, but things went sour when Allie grew really tall and Chris didn't grow at all. Between the short jokes and the superstar attitude, neither Chris nor I had much use for Allie.

"Dad wants Allie to have a long workout," I said, digging through the dishwasher for a clean spoon. "And reporters are supposed to be there."

Chris made a face at his pudding. Just then the phone

rang. It was my dad, calling from the field on his cellular phone.

"Mol?"

"Ymmm," I said, my mouth full of sweet, creamy tapioca.

"Your sister's mouth hurts. Could you hop on your bike and bring a bag of ice to the field?"

"Can't she wait until Mom gets out of work? Chris and I are supposed to—"

"No. She can't." He clicked the phone off and I hung up my end. I rolled my eyes at Chris.

"So what does the great one need this time?" he asked, licking the last of the pudding out of his bowl.

"Ice." I pouted. "Her teeth hurt."

"Imagine that," Chris said. "The pain-in-the-butt has a pain in the mouth."

"Yeah, imagine that." I dumped a tray of ice cubes into a plastic bag and imagined what it would be like to have the world revolve around me.

Chris and I arrived at the field ten minutes later. The grass was a deep green and the infield was raked clean and bordered with sharp white lines. Pulling in the parking lot behind us was a silver van with "Channel 7" painted on the side and a small satellite dish on its roof.

"Ah, man," Chris whined. "TV's here? Just to see Allie?"

"Are you kidding?" I said. "My dad's been planning this for months." We dropped our bikes at the fence and trotted over to the dugout. My hand was freezing from the bag of ice.

"Here," I said, holding it out to Dad and dripping water onto his score book.

"Molly," he snapped. "Be careful."

"Sorry."

"Just hold that for me until Allie comes back from the bathroom," he said as he studied his lineup. Chris and I slumped onto the bench and watched the ice melt and the Channel 7 crew unpack their van. A big man in a suit made his way across the outfield toward us.

"Hey, Tom!" the reporter shouted.

Dad jumped up to meet him. "Mike. Thanks for coming."

Chris's eyes bugged out as the man drew closer. "Is that—?"

"Yeah," I said. "Mike Cronin. He used to catch for the Yankees."

"Friend of your dad's?" Chris whispered.

"Fan of Allie's," I said.

"Yuck," Chris said. "Stopped too many pitches with his helmet, I guess."

I snickered. Dad flashed me a quick frown out of the smile he had plastered on his face for the camera. "Go find Allie," Dad said out of the side of his mouth. "I want to get this interview done before any other players get here. We don't want any distractions, do we?"

I rolled my eyes at Chris, and we headed for the Porta-Potty in search of my sister.

By June the Porta-Potties are unbearable. Hot days, lots of people using them—the smell is enough to make the freckles fall off my face. In April, on Opening Day,

I suppose the giant plastic outhouses are still bearable. Even so, Allie had been in there for at least ten minutes, which had to be a Brookdale record.

I pounded on the door. "Allie?" I called. No answer. I banged again. "Hey, Allie!"

"Gah wah," she said.

"What?" I asked, raising my eyebrows at Chris. He shrugged; he had no clue either.

"Gab lass," she screamed.

The words were garbled but the tone was clear. Annoyed.

"Allie, why are you talking funny?" I asked.

"Ah'm nah tackin funny," she said.

Chris howled. "She sounds like she's chewing on her glove."

I shushed him. "Allie, you gotta come out. The TV people are here," I said.

She screamed something like "Shic you hed dun a fwog strat," which probably meant "Stick your head down a frog's throat." That's Allie's favorite saying.

I ran over to Dad and tugged on the sleeve of his silky red Blazer jacket as he talked to Mike Cronin.

"Hey, Dad. Allie's foaming at the mouth," I whispered.

"Excuse me, Mike," Dad said, then leaned down to me. "What are you talking about, Molly?"

"She won't come out of the Porta-Potty."

"Stop fooling around and get your sister over here," Dad hissed, then turned back to Mike with a TV smile. "She's on her way."

Mike Cronin put his hand on my shoulder and I

7

stopped short. "Wait a minute," he said. "Is this Allie's sister?"

"This is Molly," Dad said. "She's ten."

Mike Cronin squatted down next to me. He was thick and strong, and I could imagine him pounding his mitt and waiting for a ninety-mile-an-hour fastball.

"Are you a superstar, too?" he asked.

I gulped, not knowing what to say. I looked up at Dad.

"She's working at it," Dad said. "Go get Allie," he snapped. "Mr. Cronin doesn't have all day."

Neither do I, I wanted to say. Instead, I ran back and knocked on the green plastic door again.

"Allie, a reporter's here to see you."

"I'm nah givin intafews," she mumbled through the door. Must be nice to be important enough to give interviews, let alone refuse to give them. But how would I know?

"What do you mean, she's not coming out?" Dad said. Mike Cronin and his cameraman were setting up near the pitcher's rubber to film Allie's warm-ups.

I shrugged and followed Dad over to the Porta-Potty.

Chris was waiting far enough away that he couldn't smell the outhouse, and studying his watch. "Twenty minutes," Chris whispered. "No one's ever been in one of those that long."

"She'll come out slimy green," I whispered back. Then we both burst with laughter.

Dad turned sharply. "You better not upset your sister. You know how sensitive she is."

"Yeah, about as sensitive as my dirty sneakers," I

said to Chris under my breath. Then we laughed again.

"They're laffin' ah me," Allie screeched from inside the Porta-Potty.

"Stop it," Dad snapped.

"I didn't do anything," I protested.

Dad glared at me. "If she doesn't pitch well tonight, I'm going to hold you personally responsible, Molly." I wanted to glare back, but I was afraid if I narrowed my eyes, tears would squeeze out.

Dad turned to the Porta-Potty and knocked lightly. "Sweetheart, come on out. We've got to start your warm-up."

"Na!" she shouted through the door.

"Why not, Allie?"

"Ah luk stoopih."

"Allie, no one cares how you look. All they care about is your fastball."

Lucky Allie. At least she had a fastball.

Mike Cronin left after half an hour without getting the interview he had waited for all winter. Dad told some lame story about Allie having pregame jitters and suggested they could just film the game from a distance. The Blazers began to arrive at the field. They were ready for Opening Day in their bright red shirts with a streak of gold lightning and flaming "Blazers" across the front. Dad grabbed Jeni and Kristin and sent them over to the Porta-Potty.

Jeni and Kristin were the two best players on the Blazers, not counting Allie, of course. Kristin was small and quick like a rabbit. Dad said she was the best shortstop in the state. Jeni was tall, even taller than Allie, but without the sharp edges. She was a lefty, so Dad used her at first. But Dad didn't pick them for this job because of their talent. They both had braces.

They knocked at the door and talked low into the crack around the hinges. I couldn't tell what they were saying because Dad had sent Chris and me to the bleachers, with firm orders not to move an inch. We saw the door to the Porta-Potty open and Allie's long arm reach out and drag Jeni and Kristin inside.

The opposing team, the Fever, took the field for warm-ups. The stands began to fill with people. Two newspaper reporters appeared with notebooks and cameras. Dad gave the Blazers a last-minute pep talk and turned his head every thirty seconds to look out at the Porta-Potty. Chris timed the girls on his watch: Allie had been in for an hour—that was world record one—and the three of them were in together for fifteen minutes—world record two. "It's just not healthy breathing Porta-Potty air," Chris warned. "They'll start a plague or something."

At one minute before game time Jeni and Kristin came out, waving their hands in front of their faces. Jeni looked back and yelled something as the door slammed behind her. Dad trotted across the outfield and through the back gate. I could hear him shouting from across the field. "Forget it," he yelled. "We've got a game to play. If Allie doesn't want to pitch, I'll find someone else."

He turned back toward the infield and Kristin and Jeni followed. As he reached second base the door to the Porta-Potty opened and Allie stuck her head out. Dad glanced over his shoulder, then kept walking as if he hadn't seen her. Allie stumbled along behind him, her hat pulled down over her face. As she walked through the outfield toward the mound, a small group of Blazers' parents noticed her and began to applaud. Other fans turned to look and soon the bleachers on both sides were rocking with people cheering for Allie. She didn't look up, but she touched her cap, then gave a little wave.

Dad waited for her at the pitcher's circle. She reached out her hand and he handed her a bright white softball. He patted her on the shoulder and trotted back to the dugout.

With her mouth tightly shut, Allie threw a few warm-up pitches. Then the ump yelled "Play ball!" and Allie lifted her head. The first batter stepped into the box and Allie stared at her, then flashed a smile shining with braces and victory.

Chapter Two

Allie pitched a two-hitter that Opening Day. Not her best game ever, but Channel 7 loved it. With her fastball blazing and her braces sparkling, she was the lead story of *Sports at 11.*

"See," said Mom to Dad. "I told you she could pitch with braces."

"See," said Dad to Allie. "I told you, you could pitch with braces."

"Sheah," said Allie to Kristin and Jeni. "I tad yah he'd make mah pitch—effin if I was dyun."

"See," I said to Chris. "I told you they were all boring."

First of all, Allie strikes almost everyone out, so the fielders just swat mosquitoes and kick dirt for six innings. Second, Dad has the Blazers trained better than the marines. You never get any interesting errors like two runners on the same base or the second baseman booting the ball into the outfield.

I wanted to play for the Blazers this spring. I wasn't alone; since the Blazers won the championship last year, every girl in Brookdale wanted to be on the team. But I was the only girl in Brookdale—except for Allie, of course—who was the coach's daughter. I thought I was a sure bet to make the team.

Tryouts had been held at the end of a snowy February in the high school gym. That night I asked Dad if I made his team.

"You're only ten," Dad said. "That's a bit young for Majors."

"Allie was in Majors when she was ten," I said.

Dad twiddled with his mustache and sighed. "It's better for you to stay in Minors another year. Get some more experience."

I felt a worm digging in my stomach. How much more experience could I get? I had been in Minors, the 10-and-under division, for two years. At the rate I was going, I wouldn't make the 12-and-under Majors until I was forty-six. I walked away in case the worm feeling made me cry. I sat on the back stairs and listened to Mom continue the discussion in the kitchen.

"Tom, Molly is ready to play Majors. She did great in tryouts."

"Diane, the Blazers' roster is filled," Dad said.

"How can it be filled? Two girls from last year moved up to Seniors," Mom said.

"Alyssa Hagan and Erin Cohen are joining the team."

"Alyssa? She plays for the Crush. And wasn't Erin

on the Thunder?" I could hear Mom sigh. "How did you steal them away from their teams, Tom?"

There was a long silence. I could hear Dad tapping his pencil on the countertop.

"Well, Tom? What strings did you pull?"

"No strings, Diane. Alyssa's parents both work and Erin's mom is a single parent. The only way the girls could get to softball practice is to hitch a ride with a neighbor, who happens to be Kristin. So they asked to be traded to the Blazers."

"Honestly, Tom, you should be ashamed of yourself. It's bad enough you stole two top-notch players from other teams. But you squeezed out Molly's spot on the roster." I could hear pots banging and drawers slamming. Mom was ripping mad.

"I have to do what's best for Allie," Dad said. "The Nationals are within reach, Diane. It's the opportunity of a lifetime for her."

"What about Molly?" Mom asked.

"Let Molly stay in Minors and have the time she needs to develop," Dad said.

What was Dad waiting for me to develop into? My sister? I would never be as good as her. So I figured I would never be good enough for Dad.

I went to bed and buried my head in my pillow.

The next day Mr. Sinnott, the director of the Minor Leagues, called me and told me I was on the Cookie Monsters. I thought I would die of embarrassment. Last year I played on the Firecats. How could I be on a team named Cookie Monsters? Then he told me that Mick Pimental would be my coach.

"But he coaches Majors—the Sting," I said. The Sting were the Brookdale town champs every year—until two years ago when ten-year-old Allie Burrows arrived in Majors and swept everyone away, including the mighty Sting.

"Mick wants to work with younger girls this year," Mr. Sinnott explained.

Mick Pimental was a legend in Brookdale. He had been coaching softball forever, developing strong teams and strong players. He and Dad had been rivals since Dad came to Majors. Dad was not amused when I told him who my coach was.

"Isn't that great?" Mom said.

"He's a bad role model," he said at her through gritted teeth.

"He's a good coach," she said, biting the inside of her cheeks so she wouldn't laugh. I knew she must have pulled some strings of her own.

The Cookie Monsters opened their season two nights after the Blazers' first game. I was so excited I changed into my uniform right after school, even though game time wasn't until six P.M. I was ready to conquer the world until I made the mistake of going into the family room. Allie, Jeni, and Kristin were gathered around the TV, wolfing down popcorn and orange juice. Jeni and Kristin just ignored me, as usual, but Allie's eyes popped out at my bright blue shirt with "Cookie Monsters" scrolled in white letters across the front. She snickered, then twitched, then laughed.

"Cookie Monsters?" she said, gulping for air. "Your team is called 'Cookie Monsters'?"

Typical. I've been practicing for three weeks and she never even asked me what team I was on.

"So what," I said. Jeni and Kristin turned to look at me and my face went hot.

"When I played Minors, I was on the Terminators," Allie said.

"Hey, I was on the Pressure," Jeni said.

"So what," I said again. I could feel the red rising in my face. I hate when that happens. I have red hair and I don't like to be the same color all over.

"No one is going to respect a team called"—Allie yukked like a sick goose—"Cookie Monsters." Jeni and Kristin began yukking and I felt like I was in a barnyard. I wished they would all throw up. Goose vomit. Though with my luck, I'd be the one who had to clean it up because they were too busy being softball stars.

As soon as Mom dropped me off at the field, I ran to Mick to see if we could change the team's name.

"We're stuck with it, kiddo," he said. "There was a mix-up in sizes when the League ordered the uniforms. One of the T-ball teams is wearing teeny, weeny Pirates' shirts. You bigger girls get to be Cookie Monsters. No big deal."

"No big deal?" I said. "It's a baby name!" Just then the scoreboard lit up in center field. *Bombers vs. Cookie Monsters.* I wanted to crawl into the bat bag.

"We don't need a tough name to be a tough team,"

16

he growled and waved us onto the field for warm-ups.

We batted and fielded and ran and by game time I knew he was right. I felt so great I could have been wearing a wedding dress and I wouldn't have cared. It was Opening Day! Sure, there were no TV cameras. But the bleachers on both sides were buzzing with people, and I could smell the pizza and sausages grilling at the snack bar. The public address system was whining with Mr. Sinnott's "one-two-three testing, is this darn thing working yet?" and kids were running in and out of the bleachers, playing tag.

Allie was around somewhere. It's a family rule that we have to go to each other's games. She was probably playing catch with one of her stuck-up Blazers friends or getting free hot dogs at the snack bar. They give her whatever she wants because she's so famous.

Chris perched at the top of the bleachers, giving me long-distance high fives. He and I always go to each other's games. Except we do it because we want to, not because our parents make us. Last night had been his opening day with his baseball team, the Marlins, and I had been there for every pitch, cheering him on. Just like I knew he would do for me tonight.

Behind the fence, next to our dugout, Mom and Dad sat in lawn chairs ready to watch me play the best game in the world—fast-pitch softball.

And I was ready to play my heart out. Even if it was for a team named Cookie Monsters.

Chapter Three

The Cookie Monsters were home team, so we took the field first. We put away the Bombers one-two-three in the top of the first. When we got up to bat, Katie, our leadoff batter, struck out. As Mindy stepped in, I went into the on-deck circle.

I stretched my arms and swung my bat and squished my face to look menacing. Dad hissed at me behind the fence. "Molly, bend your knees a little more."

I took another swing. Dad hissed again. "Pull the bat back a little."

By now Mindy had one strike and three balls on her. My hands began to sweat.

"Molly, close up your stance."

Ball four for Mindy. She went to first and I was up.

"Send it for a ride, Mol!" Dad yelled.

Mick called time and waved me over to the first-base coaching box.

"Look kiddo, when your dad tells you to do your homework, you open those books. He tells you to wash the dishes, they sparkle. But when you're on this field, you listen to me. Okay?"

I was too busy staring at him to listen to anything. Mick has a two-inch-long cigar that's about fifty years old. He keeps it clenched in his teeth but he never lights it because coaches should never smoke in front of kids. So he chews on it, bouncing it up and down between his lips every time he yells. When he goes onto the field he has to hide it, so he can't be accused of displaying tobacco inside the white lines.

I found out where he hid it. He puffed his cheeks and I saw the cigar sliming around inside his mouth.

"Now, Molly, do you remember the signs?"

I nodded my head yes, wondering if he ever swallowed one. A cigar, I mean.

"Good. Get back there and do a good job."

I settled back into the batter's box. I heard Dad: "Come on, Mol, smash it." I heard Chris, squeaking out a "Whoa, Molly." I couldn't hear Mom but I knew she was praying under her breath: "Please let her hit it."

Mick swiped his hand across his chest. That's a take. So I settled in and let the first pitch pass me by. Strike one, but Mindy stole second. I looked at Mick again. He touched his cap twice then leaned forward with his hands on his knees. Bunt.

I squared around. The ball was high and I tipped it foul. Mick patted his left shoulder. Hit away. I tightened my hands on the bat and peered out at the center field fence. I didn't care if I was only ten years old and I still needed time to develop. I was going to take the ball downtown. Home run.

The pitch came in a little high, just how I like it. I stepped forward, pulled my arms around, snapped my wrists and hit—air.

"Strike three!" called the umpire. Chris called, "Nice cut." Mom mumbled, "Next time, Mol."

My dad just groaned.

The game had its ups and downs. I walked twice and stole second both times. I scored a run when Sylvia De-Marco hit a steaming single to right. I played shortstop the whole game and didn't bobble the ball once. I threw five runners out at first and one at home. One time I did overthrow first base. The ball flew into the stands and crashed through someone's Styrofoam cooler. Chris said a two-liter bottle of soda exploded fizz all over the crowd. Mick said I had the strongest arm he had ever seen in a kid my age. Needed some work, though.

We were tied 6–6 going into the bottom of the last inning. Katie and Mindy struck out quickly, leaving me as the last hope to avoid a tie.

I hadn't gotten a hit yet. I looked over at Mick, thinking he might want to put in a pinch hitter. He smiled and patted his left shoulder. Hit away.

"Come on, Mol," Chris called. "You can do it."

"Do your best, sweetheart," Mom urged. Big deal. She tells me that when I'm brushing my teeth.

Dad didn't say anything.

My hands started to shake, so I stepped out of the

box and pretended to knock the dirt out of my cleats. I stepped back in and took a ball. My hands felt sweaty, so I rubbed them in the dirt. I looked at Mick. Hit away.

The ball came in fast and low. I slammed it. I flew to first base and took the turn just in time to see the ball clear the left field fence—way to the left of the pole. Foul ball.

"Wow," Mom said, jumping up for my long strike one.

"Do it again," Mick urged.

"Straighten it out," Dad demanded.

The pitcher stepped off the rubber and took a deep breath. She was the one sweating now.

Then I heard a creaky voice singing "Cookie, cookie, cookie." I looked down at the catcher. Even through her mask, I could see her stupid grin. I sneered and the pitch danced past me. Strike two.

The catcher walked the ball out to the pitcher. They whispered and giggled. The catcher gloated as she came back to home plate. "I just told her not to be afraid of a Muppet."

I tried to glare. I blushed instead. I hate it, turning red all the time.

The catcher settled back in and starting singing that "cookie, cookie, cookie" song. I was so mad I missed the pitch going by. A ball. I heard Chris call out "Good eye." Good luck was more like it.

Every time the catcher sang "cookie" I snarled back "monster." I let the next pitch go by. Definitely high and outside.

The next pitch came in low and fast. I swung hard and low, too low, I realized at the last moment. But I caught a piece of it. I ran like I was on fire. It felt so terrific that I ignored Mick's signal to stop at first. I sped to second base and slid into the second baseman. She and the ball hit the dust, so I jumped up and ran again.

The girl coaching third stood there with her mouth open. I tagged the base and took the turn to home. I heard Dad and Mom and Chris and Mick all yelling "Slide!" I flung myself headfirst and heard a loud "clunk."

Chris told me later that I got hit on the helmet with the throw coming in from the shortstop. I didn't care because all I heard was the umpire yelling "Safe!" and the crowd cheering and clapping. Mick high-fived me and said, "Good job. But we'll have to talk about missed signs later."

My teammates jumped all over me. Our first game, our first win. We were number one!

We lined up to shake hands with the Bombers. As I passed by their catcher, I couldn't help myself. "Bomb, bomb, bomb. Bombers got bombed!"

Afterward, I ran over to see Mom while Dad went to the snack bar for coffee. Allie slouched down in a lawn chair, munching on a hamburger—no doubt a free one.

"What a wonderful run, Molly," Mom gushed.

"It won the game!"

"Sure did!" She hugged me and went over to get Dad away from all his softball buddies clustered at the snack bar.

I just couldn't stop talking about it. "Hey, Allie.

Wasn't that neat? My first hit of the season was a home run!"

Allie slowly stood, unfolding those spider arms and legs. She looked down at me with her cold blue eyes. "You swung for a ball, not a strike. Then you got a lucky single, followed by three errors."

My happiness fizzled like a leaky balloon. "So who died and made you official scorekeeper?" I yelled as she walked away.

She turned and smirked. "If you were on the Blazers, Dad would chew you out for not stopping at first base. He wouldn't congratulate you for a bogus home run. Which was only a pitiful single anyway."

"You're just jealous because I did something good for once!"

Her eyes widened and she started laughing. She laughed all the way to the parking lot.

I didn't feel like I was number one any more.

Chapter Four

The next Saturday was sunny and spring-breezy. Chris and I played catch in his front yard. We have this rule: if we play in his yard, we play baseball; in my yard, it's softball. Chris was doing a lot of pitching for the Marlins, so I squatted in the catcher's crouch, giving him a target to practice with. He was throwing some hot strikes when we were interrupted by a tremendous snort. Without looking, I knew Allie had arrived.

"What do you want?" I stood up to stretch my legs.

Allie snorted again. My sister has the vocabulary of a groundhog.

"Is there something we can do for you?" Chris asked.

"You've already done it. Given me a good laugh, watching you try—" Allie snorted a third time—"to pitch." Someday my sister is going to strangle herself with her snorts.

I threw the ball back to Chris and crouched down.

Chris gave me a quick flick with his head. No way would he pitch while Allie was around. So we tossed the ball back and forth, ignoring my sister. After a few moments she spoke, this time like a human instead of a chimpanzee.

"Hey, Mol. You're in the newspaper."

"No kidding?" I spoke too fast, wishing a second later I hadn't been so eager.

"Right here in the sports section."

Allie unfolded the *Brookdale Times* and showed me my first press clipping ever. Allie, of course, had a scrapbook full of them.

> The Cookie Monsters beat the Bombers, 7–6, with a solid single by Molly Burrows, who took advantage of three Bomber errors to score the winning run.

"See," she gloated. "I told you it was only a single."

I shoved the newspaper at her. "Get lost. Mars would be good."

"Not so fast," she answered. "Since I was kind enough—"

I snorted this time.

"—to walk all the way over here with the newspaper, the least you can do is look at the article about me."

Chris tapped my arm. "Look at it," he whispered, "or we'll never get rid of her."

Allie flipped back to page two of the Sports section:

Blazers Win Opener
Burrows Pitches 2-Hitter

"You're wonderful, Allie," said Chris, then pretended to throw up. "Come on, Mol."

"Wait!" Allie said. She folded away the Sports section and pulled out the front page of the paper. "Look at this."

We followed her pointing finger to a box at the bottom of the page:

ALLIE TALLY

Watch every Saturday for an update on Brookdale's speed queen, Allie Burrows. Here's how she looks after Week 1 of the season:

GP	2
Won	2
Lost	0
Ks	26
BBs	2
ERA	0.00

Here's what it all meant: Allie pitched two games (GP) and won both. She had twenty-six strike-outs (Ks) and had walked only two batters (BBs are bases on balls). She hadn't given up a run (ERA is earned run average). Allie was a sensation and the *Brookdale Times* was going to make sure everyone knew about it.

I wanted to throw up.

It was bad enough that the world revolved around Allie. But did she have to rub my face in it every chance she got? As Allie strutted back across the street to our house, I cursed her with a thousand disasters.

"Like what?" Chris wanted to know.

"Something terrible," I said, feeling the tears in my throat. Chris and I have a no-crying rule, so I bit them back.

"Like what?" he asked, tossing me the ball.

"Warts on her pitching hand!" I whipped the ball back.

"Not disgusting enough," he said. "How about warts all over, including her armpits, her elbows, and up her nose? Brown, black, and orange ones, with hair growing out of them."

"Wow," I said. Chris was good. "Warts all over her body including in her nasal passages." Unlike my sister, I have an excellent vocabulary.

"Is that the same as her nose?" Chris asked.

"Yeah. Let's see how well she snorts with a noseful of warts."

"Okay. What else?"

"Isn't a wart curse enough?"

"Not for Allie." Years of Allie's short jokes had made Chris hungry for revenge.

"The wart stuff," I said, thinking hard. "Plus I wish she'd wake up and find out that her braces had stuck together, so she couldn't open her mouth."

"Come on, Mol. Put your heart into it." He walked over and put his hand on my shoulder. "Make the braces barbed wire."

"Barbed wire?" I tried to picture Allie with a mouth that could stop a horse.

"Yeah! With big chunks of food stuck in them."

"You mean like poppy seeds?" I asked. Mrs. Reid, our science teacher, always has a bagel for coffee break and we spend fourth period watching her pick poppy seeds out of her teeth.

"Bigger!"

"Okay." I took a deep breath. "I curse my sister, Allison-the-Ego Burrows, with warts all over her body and with braces liked barbed wire. Rusty barbed wire. Stuck with corncobs and spareribs and wads of gum and—" I stopped. I was making myself sick.

Chris pitched in. "And sauerkraut and pigs' feet and radishes that no amount of brushing or flossing will ever remove."

"Yes!" I cried as Chris and I leaped into the air, twirled around, and came down in our special hand-shake. That's what I like about Chris. He always brings out the best in me.

Chapter Five

It was about three weeks later that Allie's next disaster struck. Softball season was in full swing. The Blazers were blowing everyone away in the 12-and-under division. The Allie Tally was astounding:

```
        ALLIE TALLY

Allie sizzles!
        GP    10
        Won   10
        Lost  0
        Ks    126
        BBs   24
        ERA   0.13
```

Whenever Allie pitched, the stands were packed. Families and friends, coaches from other leagues, reporters, and people from all over our corner of California flocked to Brookdale to see the great Allison Burrows. Dad said even college coaches were talking about scholarships. Mom said let's get Allie out of sixth grade first.

The Cookie Monsters were in first place, too. But who cared—we were Minors. Developing players were of no interest to anyone.

The night the disaster occurred, the Blazers were playing the Sting for the first time that spring. Mick's old team was also undefeated, led by an excellent pitcher named Meghan King. Channel 7 and Channel 4 had sent camera crews. Even Chris and I decided to watch the game for a change, instead of hanging out at the playground. I was dying to see the Blazers get creamed and Mick said Meghan was the girl who could do it.

The stands were packed. Chris and I were about to give up on finding a seat when I spotted Mick sitting at the scorekeeper's table behind the backstop. I strolled over to the scorekeeper with a sad pout on my face.

"Excuse me," I said.

Mick glanced over at me. "Hi, Mol."

"Hi, Mr. Pimental."

"Here to see Allie pitch?"

I dropped my lip lower. "We can't find a place to sit."

The scorekeeper looked at me closely. "You're Allison Burrows's sister, aren't you?"

I nodded sweetly.

"You don't look a thing like her," she said as she studied me. People always said that. Allie was tall and skinny, while I was short and sturdy. Allie has black hair like Mom's. I have red hair like Dad's. She was a champion. I was a kid.

"If you saw her play, you'd know she was Allie's sister," Mick growled. Goose bumps danced on my arm. Why couldn't Dad talk about me like that?

The scorekeeper smiled. "Well, why don't you and your friend slide right in here under the table. You won't be in anyone's way and you'll have the best seats in the house!"

"Thanks," I yelped, and Chris and I dived into the dust. I couldn't wait for Dad to see me sitting at Mick's feet.

The Sting were home team, so they took the field first. Meghan struck out Lauren, Jeni, and Kristin with nine hot pitches. My stomach felt like a worm had died there, and I was suddenly glad that Dad hadn't wanted me for the Blazers. Meghan was scary.

Allie was even scarier.

All those years I spent at the ball fields, all those years Mom forced me to sit around while the crowds applauded my sister—I never really paid attention. But when I saw Allie throw that night against the Sting, I finally understood. My sister threw harder and faster than any girl I had ever seen.

I studied each pitch. First she brings her hands together with the ball in the glove. It's called presenting the ball. She leans forward slightly and then swings her arm forward and up to begin the windmill motion.

Halfway through the circle her arm is moving like a roller coaster barreling downhill. This is known as arm speed; Allie's got a lot of it.

At the same time her arm is coming around, she kicks her left foot out hard and high, causing her to leap toward the batter. Her wrist and her hip snap together and the ball explodes out of her hand. She finishes her leap and the batter has to contend with both the pitch and Allie coming straight at her.

Really scary.

At the other end of Allie's delivery is Sumner Comeau. She's been Allie's catcher since they were eight years old. Last year Dad bought Sumner a foam glove to wear under her catcher's mitt. Even so, after Sumner warmed up Allie, she shook her glove hand behind her back as if trying to shake out the smart.

Allie sat down the Sting in the bottom of the first. The game was a pitching duel until the bottom of the fourth. Allie was the leadoff batter and Dad gave her a series of signs from the first-base coaching box.

"That's the bunt sign," Mick whispered under the table.

I whipped my head around. "You know my dad's signs?" I asked.

"Yup," said Mick.

Dad would croak if he knew that.

Sure enough, Allie squared around and bunted. She hustled to first, becoming the first base runner in the game. She assumed the sprinter's position, ready to race to second.

"Watch for a pitchout now," Mick whispered.

Meghan pitched the ball high and outside. There it was—the pitchout. Her catcher snagged it and fired it to second. Allie stealing a base is not a pretty sight—toothpick legs pumping, elbows flying, ponytail bouncing. As the throw came in, Allie dived headfirst and held on to the bag.

"Safe!" yelled the ump.

"No headfirst slides!" roared my father. "You want to hurt your pitching hand?"

Have you seen those bronze baby shoes that parents get made of their baby's first walking shoes? That's what Dad's going to do with Allie's pitching hand someday.

Sumner was up next.

"Watch for the hit-and-run," Mick said. "With a runner on second, a ground ball could knock in a run." The Sting coach moved his infielders in front of the base paths.

"How come he's pulling them in short?" Chris asked.

"To knock down a ground ball and keep Allie from scoring," Mick said.

On the first pitch, Allie sprinted toward third and Sumner swung at the ball. It was a real low pitch—Mick said Meghan was trying to force Sumner into a pop-up. A fly ball on a hit-and-run is an almost certain double play. But Sumner lucked out; the ball bounced over the infield, a short single. Allie flew around third and scored that important first run.

Laura Ramon was the next Blazers' batter. Meghan threw another pitchout, expecting Sumner to dash toward second. Dad held her at first.

"Your father won't hold her a second time," Mick said.

Sure enough, Dad had Laura take the next pitch and Sumner flew off the base. The Sting catcher made a bullet throw and the shortstop was waiting. Sumner threw herself headfirst and sent the shortstop spinning.

"Out!" yelled the umpire. As the dust settled, Sumner picked herself up.

Dad called time and trotted out to her. "Do not slide into a base headfirst! Don't you know—"

He stopped. Sumner's shoulders hunched up. She lifted her hand up to show Dad something. Then he bellowed, "Get the first-aid kit! And some ice!"

"I don't like the looks of this," Mick said in a low voice.

Sumner's knees bent and she began to slump to the ground. Dad caught her and carried her to the dugout. The girls gathered around her. Dad waved them away.

Sumner's parents ran to the dugout, then her father raced to the parking lot and drove his car onto the field. Sumner sat up again; her face was now a pasty white. Her arm was wrapped in a towel and someone had used an Ace bandage to wrap it against her chest.

Her parents helped her into the car and drove her away. The coaches and the ump tried to get the girls back into the game. No one moved very fast.

I pushed my way down toward the dugout to see what had happened.

"Allie!" I hissed.

"Get out of here," she snapped and headed to the far side of the dugout.

34

"Rhianna!" Rhianna Polaski came over to the fence.

"What happened to Sumner?" I asked.

"You mean you don't know?"

"We couldn't see from where we were."

Rhianna bit back tears. "She broke her arm. You could see the bone under her skin."

I felt sick.

Behind her, the Blazers picked up their gloves to go out to the field. Dad called out: "Who wants to catch?"

No one volunteered.

Chapter Six

The next day's headlines said it all: Burrows Stung for Loss.

After Sumner had been carted off to the hospital, Dad emptied the bench trying to find a catcher for Allie.

Kristin was Dad's first recruit. She snagged all of Allie's fastballs. But since she was tiny for a twelve-year-old, each pitch sent her flying onto her butt. Jeni was the next one to put on the catcher's gear. The shin pads didn't fit her long legs and she stopped a fireball with her thigh. She spent the rest of the game on the bench, icing a lump the size of a grapefruit.

Dad went through the whole roster—from Lauren, his center fielder, to Rhianna Polaski, the Blazers' bench warmer, who made the team mostly because her dad was the assistant coach and a former professional baseball player.

No one could catch my sister.

By the top of the sixth, the Sting were ahead 5–1. No one had gotten a hit off Allie but there were so many passed balls—pitches that a catcher should catch but doesn't—that the Sting ran around the base paths like rabbits. The Blazers managed only four hits off Meghan.

After the game Allie slammed her glove on the ground and stomped off the field.

"Allie!" Dad called.

"Let her go," urged my mom.

"We've got a problem, Tom," said Mr. Polaski. "We need a catcher."

"I know."

"What are you going to do about it?"

Dad shook his head. "I don't know."

Dad spent Friday and Saturday trying to arrange a trade.

"Barbara, it's Tom Burrows. Oh, you heard about Sumner Comeau. She's fine, but she's out for the season. That's why I'm calling . . ."

Dad got so desperate he even offered to trade Lauren, Jeni, and Kristin for a catcher. They were players any coach would kill for. But there were no nibbles. Mom said Dad was getting his comeuppance.

"Why do you say that?" I asked.

"For three years your dad's been scooping up all the talent and leaving the other coaches to struggle," she explained. "They're getting back at him."

I figured Allie was getting her comeuppance, too, and I wanted to rub it in. I found her sitting in a black cloud in the family room, fists clenched in her lap. I decided to save her comeuppance for some other time.

Dad came in, worn out from his calls. He flung the phone book into a drawer and slouched onto the sofa.

"Dad?" Allie said.

"Don't worry, honey. I'll get you a catcher," Dad promised.

"How?" Allie wanted to know. "No one wants to trade with the Blazers."

"I'm going to take a look at the younger girls tonight at Molly's game."

Allie snorted and wrapped herself back in her black cloud.

The Cookie Monsters were playing the Lightning that night. Actually, we were now just the Monsters, since I had persuaded Mick to let us peel "Cookie" off our shirts. I was determined to play an excellent game— no missed signals, no throws into the stands, and after what had happened to Sumner, no headfirst slides. Maybe while Dad was looking for talent, he'd look my way. Sure, I wasn't a catcher, but I figured he could train one of the other girls and slip me into her position.

We'd beaten the Lightning twice already, so we expected to be in for an easy time. We coasted until Beth Tucker came to bat in the second inning. Beth had moved to town from Arizona just a week earlier and was in my fourth grade class. I told her how to sign up for softball.

My mistake.

We were ahead 3–0. Stephanie Fitzpatrick was pitching for the Monsters and I was at shortstop. Beth let the first pitch go by, yawning as the ball came through the strike zone. Strike one.

She looked somewhat interested at the next pitch, a soft low one. Strike two. Her coach yelled from the sidelines: "Beth, the strike zone! Protect that plate."

Beth smiled broadly and knocked dirt from her cleats. She stepped back in for the next pitch. Her body quivered and her feet shifted. The worm jumped in my stomach. I moved a bit to my right, just in case Beth decided to wake up and play the game.

The next pitch came in, fat and juicy, and *bam!* Beth hammered it over left field, all the way out to the parking lot. Home run. Above the cheering, I could hear Dad. "How old is that kid and where did she come from?"

The next batter slammed a line drive to my left. I snatched the ball out of the air, rolled in the dirt, and leaped up. After I flipped the ball back to Stephanie, I looked for my father. He was talking to the Lightning coach and had missed my awesome play!

I came up to bat in the fourth inning. Bases were loaded, a good time to show my stuff. I looked at Mick, expecting a hit away. Instead he gave me a take. I bugged out my eyes.

He repeated the sign, rubbing his nose, elbow, shoulder, and then the real thing—the left hand to the right ear. Take. I almost ground the bat to powder in my hands. It was my favorite pitch, high and down the middle. Out of the strike zone but sweet just the same.

Mick's next flurry of signs ended with a swipe across his chest. That means the first sign still stands! Another take? I couldn't believe it! Meanwhile, my teammates on the bench were cheering me on:

> Got three ducks on the pond,
> Want another one on.
> Get a hit quack, quack,
> Get a hit!

How could I get a hit when Mick wouldn't even let me swing? I twirled the bat in my fingertips. The ball came in and flew high against the backstop. Ball two. I was wondering if Mick would let me go for the next one when I heard him yell, "Molly! Move it!" The runner on third base was trying to steal home on the wild pitch. I jumped out of the way just in time to avoid being called for interference and to allow her to score. The other runners each advanced a base.

I turned to look for my dad. He was right behind the fence. "Keep your head in the game," he said.

I took a deep breath and stepped back in. Mick gave me two more take signs. I gritted my teeth and took a ball and a strike.

With a 3–1 count, I figured Mick would finally let me

hit away. Instead, he swiped the hand across the chest—
keep the same sign! My teammates were quacking their
little hearts out, begging me to pound one, and he
wanted me to wait for a walk.

I let the bat slide into my fingers. There was the ball,
coming in like a sweet, juicy melon. *Smack me,* it
screamed. It sailed in high, too high—ball four, if I
could resist.

I couldn't.

I swung with all my might, shoulders turning, arms
flexing, wrists snapping, legs pushing. I heard that
mighty *crack* when the bat catches the ball just right.
Then a roar from the crowd. As I raced around first, I
saw the ball sail out of the park.

My teammates went wild. Mom jumped up and
down. Chris yelped. Dad gave me a victory salute.

Mike benched me.

"How many times have I told you about paying attention to my signs? It's important to the team!" His
cigar bounced with each angry word.

I swallowed to keep the teary crinkle out of my voice.
"I am so sorry, Mr. Pimental. I must have had a spot of
dirt in my eye and missed the sign."

"You're out of the game. Give you a chance to take
care of your vision problem," he snarled.

I saw Dad heading for the dugout. I stood up and
hobbled to the Gatorade.

"Mol, why are you sitting out?"

I swigged a cup of juice. "Stepped on a rock, no big
deal."

"Oh. Okay." He leaned his face against the fence. "Nice hit, sweetheart."

"Thanks." I could feel the goose bumps on my neck. They felt good.

He went back to his chair, leaving me to wonder what he was thinking. How did I stack up against Beth Tucker? We each had hit a home run. Defensively, I had sparkled at shortstop. Out in center field Beth had no action, other than watching my home run as it winged its way out of the park. I thought I had the edge.

Until Beth put on the catcher's gear in the sixth inning.

Dad pressed his face into the chain link and watched every move she made. She snatched balls out of the dirt. She threw out a runner trying to steal third. She called out each play to her infield. Beth was an excellent catcher. That was my luck—a top-notch player from Arizona drops into Brookdale, California, just in time to spoil my chances of ever becoming a Blazer.

When she came up to bat in the last inning, I still had a faint hope. Maybe she was a catcher, but I was Tom Burrows's daughter. That had to count for something. It just had to.

Beth stepped into the batter's box from the left side. She was a rightie. What was she doing, trying to bat from her opposite side? I figured she must be a show-off. She repeated the same routine, yawning through the pitches until she had two strikes on her.

On the next pitch she quivered, and that worm in my stomach started turning flips in the Gatorade. Sure enough, *bam!* The ball was airborne. A bouncing double into left field.

Stephanie recovered to strike out two batters, ending the game at 10–4. Our win.

My loss.

Chapter Seven

Dad, Allie, and Beth spent Sunday at the ball field. The Blazers had a big game Monday night and Dad wanted Beth to be ready. "Up to speed," he said. Allie's speed was what he meant.

I spent the day saving the world.

I had planned to mope all day about how I should be on the Blazers instead of Beth. Chris hunted me down in my favorite mope spot, under the lilac trees in our side yard.

"Whatcha doin'?" he wanted to know.

"Nothing."

"Let's get a game together," he said. He had his baseball cap on backward and was chewing a wad of bubble gum—that's his uniform for Sunday stickball. We play that with a taped-up whiffle bat and a tennis ball. Everyone plays: little kids, us, sometimes Chris's mom.

I was in no mood for a crowd or a game of any kind of ball. "Nah," I said.

"What're you, sick or something?" he asked, plopping on the ground beside me.

"I'm sick of ball," I said. "Can't we do something else for a change?"

"Like what?"

"Something. Anything," I said.

"Better not be Barbies."

I gave him the longest, sloppiest raspberry I could.

"Just checking," he said. "So what do you want to do?"

"I don't know. What did we do before we got into ball?"

Chris scratched his head. "Nothing. We played little kid junk."

"Remember when we used to play explorer? I used to like that."

Chris squinted his eyes, trying to remember. "When we used to go in your backwoods and build forts and stuff and pretend we were pirates or cowboys or policemen? And Allie was always the bad guy and we'd chase her and . . ."

"Allie is not part of us anymore." I snapped the words so hard I think I almost hurt Chris's feelings.

He snapped back. "That was stupid. We weren't even allowed to leave our yards."

"We can now," I said. I looked at him and he looked back and must have realized I needed to get away.

He gave me a big smile. "Where to?"

"Anywhere. Anywhere but here," I told him.

"Sure," he said. "Let's go."

I knew I could count on Chris.

We loaded knapsacks with the essentials: juice boxes, granola bars, binoculars, jackknife, rope, and Reese's peanut butter cups. Chris tried to sneak a Frisbee in his pack, but I yanked it out. "No sports today," I insisted.

With our moms' permission, we jumped on our bikes and headed north toward Quannapoag, a YMCA camp that would be deserted in early May. When Chris, Allie, and I were just little kids, we used to go there for Kiddie Kamp. The counselors told us where to go and what to do. But now Chris and I were headed there on our own. On our way to an adventure.

I was so used to flat, open spaces—my neighborhood, the ball fields, the school playground—that all the woods and the high ground spooked me at first. Camp Quannapoag had a beach on a small lake and an open field for sports. But most of the camp land was acres of forest, rising up a small, granite-ridged mountain that we called Mount Q.

Chris and I stacked our bikes against the crafts building and ran across the field. As we entered the woods, the going was easy. The afternoon was warm and the trees were covered in tiny, bright green leaves. As we got deeper into the woods, we lost sight of the field and lake, and seemed to be wrapped in a green haze.

As the path narrowed, the woods became denser, with scrubby underbrush nipping at our legs. I wished I had worn jeans instead of shorts. Even with all the scratches I was getting, I was still excited to be doing something new.

"Wanna pretend we're Indians or something?" Chris asked. Usually he pretended he was Dennis Eckersley, star reliever for the Oakland A's.

"How about Robin Hood?" I said.

"Yeah, I call Robin," he said.

"Come on, let me be Robin," I pleaded. "Robin can be either a girl or boy."

"Who am I then?" Chris countered.

"Little John." He glared at me. He hates the word "little." I corrected myself. "Will Scarlet, Robin's right-hand man?"

"Okay." Chris scrounged in the underbrush, ducking branches and pushing through prickers as he went.

"What the heck are you looking for?" I asked, thinking he was going to find a flaming case of poison ivy. When he reappeared, he had two strong sticks and a handful of pebbles. He tossed me a stick. I caught it in one hand, a daring forest bandit ready to fight all the bad guys. He poured half the pebbles in my hand.

"Here's the gold from the greedy tax collector!" he cried.

I shoved it in my pocket and yelled, "Ahoy. Here come the sheriff's men!" I tore up the path and waved for Chris to follow. We hit the base of the mountain and began to scramble up the steep ground, grabbing boulders and trees to pull ourselves up. Soon the trees gave way to a rock fall, a stretch of large rocks and small boulders that led to the base of the rocky ridge. Breathless, I pulled Chris behind a boulder the size of a small school bus.

"Hey, Mol."

"No 'Mol' here."

Chris pulled prickers from his socks. "Robin, I think 'ahoy' is a sailor word."

"So what. We've killed all the sheriff's men, so he had to get guys from the navy!"

Chris swung up on the boulder and shouted. "Look, here they come!" Sure enough, a hundred sailors galloped up the mountain on horseback.

We jumped behind the boulder. "Fire!" I commanded as we hurled rocks down the slope, crushing our attackers. Best friends, allies forever, Will and Robin fought like heroes.

When our rock piles were exhausted, we were too, so we pulled out our drink boxes and gulped down what Chris called "forest brew."

"Here's some jerky," I said, offering Chris a granola bar.

"Jerky like Allie?" he asked, pretending to look around.

"Jerky like dried, tough meat," I said.

"Yeah, like Allie," he said and laughed.

We tucked away our empty boxes in the backpacks. Chris looked up at the ridge. It was a stone wall, towering thirty feet above us. "Wanna do it?" he asked.

"We've got to," I said. "The sheriff's coming back with his catapult and flaming balls of fire."

We hit the wall ridge running; it was a steep incline with lots of nooks for climbing. We helped each other over the rough spots and made it to the top in about twenty minutes. We stood silently for a long time, letting the spring breeze cool us while we gazed at Brookdale spread out before us like a toy village.

"Is that our neighborhood?" Chris pointed to his left. I squinted hard and could see a line of houses, with his red house and our blue house facing each other.

"Follow the road to the right," I said. "See the big patch of trees? The school's on the other side."

"Yeah, I see it. Now go past it, right and up a bit. See the water tower? And there's the park. See the ball fields?"

I didn't want to see the ball fields. But my eyes followed his pointing finger and I saw the wide fields, like little oceans of green. I squinted and could make out the backstops, rising from the fields like the masts on a sailboat. And, as clearly as if I were there, I could see Allie pitching to Beth, with Dad on the sidelines saying, "What a perfect pair you are."

I rubbed my eyes hard and saw just green again. "Let's go."

"But we just got here," Chris protested.

"While we're up here cooling off, the sheriff's robbing all the villages down by the lake!"

Chris was down the ridge in a flash. He's always been a hero at heart.

By the time we got back to the lake, the villagers had all been kidnapped by the cruel sheriff and his army of sailors in their rock-dented armor. As we hit the beach, digging into the sand to keep from being spotted, we could see the sheriff's ships sailing away.

"He's heading for the castle," I whispered. I pointed to a beach about two hundred feet down the shoreline. At the edge of the water were the dungeons, disguised as changing rooms.

"We have to rescue the people." Chris hopped up and ran low along the water. He dived into the bushes and waited for me to join him.

"How?" I asked, shaking sand out of my shorts.

"Surprise attack," he said. "Approach by water." And before I could even suggest that might not be a good idea, he ran to the edge of the water and slid in, clothes and all.

"Come on, it's warm enough," he whispered. He crept along the shoreline, taking shelter under low-hanging branches. What could I do except jump in after him? Away from the main beach, the lake bottom was gooey. With each step we sunk inches into the muck and had to lift our feet carefully, so our sneakers didn't stay stuck to the bottom.

The sheriff had set his defense up on the land side of the dungeon, never expecting Robin and her band to be making a water approach. As we neared the castle Will dropped into the water and paddled along like an alligator. He turned and looked at his fearless leader still standing upright.

"You're a big target," he said. "You'd look pretty disgusting with an arrow sticking out of you."

"Just taking a look to make sure everyone's in place."

I slid into the water next to him. My hands went down into the soft, warm muck. I could feel bits of sticks and leaves. I hoped that snakes didn't live in muck. We pulled ourselves along for the last twenty feet until we came up behind the castle. It felt so good to crawl up onto the dry bank. As we inched along the ground we left a trail of wet slime.

We put our ears against the back wall of the castle. We could hear the cries of the villagers being tortured inside. I addressed the troops. "The sheriff has a hundred men out there, armed with bows and arrows and swords and horrible weapons of destruction. We're outnumbered," I said.

"So what?" Will Scarlet asked.

"Exactly," I said. "Charge!"

Will and I were off like a shot, flying around opposite sides of the castle. I punched, I kicked, I slashed, I threw off five attackers at a time. I could hear Will's bloodcurdling cries as he demolished the bad guys. We met in the front and razzed the sheriff's men as they ran into the woods. We led the cheering villagers out to the fresh air and freedom.

It was an exhausting victory, and Will and I collapsed out front. It was then that I noticed crimson streaks on his legs.

"You're bleeding," I said.

"Of course I'm bleeding," he said. "I just fought the battle of my life."

"Chris, I mean like you're really bleeding. Look at your legs!"

He looked at red trickling down his legs. Then he looked at me.

"You're bleeding, too!"

"Must be from those scratches we got in the woods." I ran over to the water and splashed my legs, trying to clear away some of the muck. As I did the blood ran more freely. I followed one stream up over my knee, where it sprung from a little hunk of mud on my thigh. I tried to brush it off but it stuck. As I looked at it more closely, I realized it was squirming.

I screamed. Like a silly crybaby.

"What!" Chris shouted. "What's the matter?"

"Bloodsucker!" I yelled. I grabbed a stick and tried to yank the creature before it sucked me dry.

Chris splashed water down his legs. "Cool," he said, "I've got four of 'em." He didn't even try to pull them off. Meanwhile, I was gouging my leg, trying to pry off the squishy brown monster that was drinking my blood. Chris came over and looked at me in envy.

"You've got at least six. Oh, Mol, here's another one!" he said happily, pulling down my wet sock.

"Get them off me!" I ordered. "Now!"

Chris pinched one and pulled gently. It came off and didn't hurt at all. He held it up, a soft wormy thing that curled around his finger. He flicked it in the water and pulled off another one.

"I'll do the rest," I said, embarrassed about my screaming fit.

"The sheriff is a crafty one," Will Scarlet said as he picked the monsters off his legs. "Leaving behind a nest of poisonous snakes."

"Yeah," I answered. "But I've got the snake serum back at our campsite."

We ran at top speed back to the beach and dug the antidote out of the knapsack. Peanut butter cups. I made sure Chris got the first dose.

I would never want to lose a friend like him.

Chapter Eight

The next day was Monday. Beth would be starting catcher for the Blazers that night. She followed me around like an itchy shadow.

"Your sister's a fantastic pitcher," she whispered in social studies.

"Your father's real nice. He knows a lot about softball," she whispered in math.

"I love the Blazers' uniforms. Red is my favorite color," she said loudly at the lunch table. I felt so sick, I threw away my chocolate cupcake.

"Allie is really nice. You must love having a sister like her," she whispered in science.

"Are you crazy?" I shouted, startling Beth and infuriating Mrs. Reid.

She glared over the top of her glasses. "Martha Burrows. Detention after school today." Detention I could handle. My real name just about killed me.

◆　◆　◆

Mom had a meeting that night, so I had to go to the field early with Dad. It was like serving a second detention. I sat in the dugout and spat sunflower seeds into a batting helmet while Dad gave the Blazers fielding practice. When I ran out of seeds, I looked up at the field and noticed Rhianna standing in at catcher. Where was Beth?

Dad was asking the same question as he brought the Blazers into the dugout. "Anybody know where Beth is?"

Lauren, in the middle of relacing her glove, looked confused. "Who's Beth?"

"Our new catcher," blurted Allie. "She's awesome. Wait till you see her."

"Let's hope we see her soon," Dad said as he scanned the parking lot. "Game starts in ten minutes. Kristin, warm Allie up. Molly, do me a favor and stack the bats."

Great, I thought. *Now I get to be bat girl for the mighty Blazers.* I opened the bat bag and dumped it. Aluminum bats on concrete make an awesome racket. Jeni gave me a dirty look.

"Tom! I need to speak with you." Harry Boucher, Director of the Majors, was at the fence. Mrs. Tucker was with him. Dad trotted over.

"Alice, is Beth all right?"

"She's fine," said Mrs. Tucker. "We really appreciate the time you spent with her yesterday. But . . ."

Mr. Boucher interrupted. "But Beth won't be playing with the Blazers." I couldn't believe what I was hearing. Neither could Dad. His mouth dropped open.

"What did you say?" he asked.

"Beth can't play on the Blazers."

"I don't understand," Dad said. I could hear the anger in the back of his throat.

"Paul Dube saw you at the field yesterday. He called to remind me that his team has the shortest roster in the Majors. If anyone gets drafted up, he gets first pick."

Dad leaned against the fence and sighed. He dug his heel into the ground, kicking up chunks of dirt.

"Allie needs her," Dad said.

"Allie has a team full of champions behind her. Paul Dube needs her more."

Dad kicked dirt and didn't answer.

"It's only fair, Tom," said Mr. Boucher.

"You're right." Dad swallowed his disappointment.

Mrs. Tucker smiled. "Beth is disappointed about not playing with the Blazers. But she's looking forward to batting against Allie."

Dad smiled. "Tell her good luck."

Mrs. Tucker handed a plastic bag to Dad and walked away. I began to lay out the catcher's gear, wondering who the heck would be wearing it.

Mr. Boucher leaned in toward Dad and lowered his voice. "Tom." My ears perked up. When a grown-up lowers his voice, he's about to say something important.

"Even with Sumner Comeau injured, there're still two other teams with shorter rosters than the Blazers. You're really not going to be able to draft from the ten-and-unders, unless . . ."

"Unless what?" Dad said.

"Unless you exercise family option and draft Molly up."

Dad turned to me and stared. I stared back. Didn't blink once. He tossed me the bag that Mrs. Tucker had left.

"Go put this on."

I looked inside the bag. There was a bright red shirt and hat—a brand new Blazer uniform.

"Move it, Molly. Game starts in three minutes."

Man, did I move it!

It wasn't until I was standing in the infield watching Allie finish her warm-ups that I realized I was the starting shortstop for the Brookdale Blazers. Not only the best team in the Majors, but last year's 12-and-under California State champs. I'd finally caught up with my sister.

Dad had sent Chris pedaling home to get my glove and cleats. Meanwhile, I was starting the game in my old Keds and using Rhianna's glove. The ump signaled Allie for the last warm-up and Kristin, suited in catcher's gear, yelled, "Coming down."

Kristin made a throw to second. I hustled left to cover the bag and crashed into something like a wall. I looked up from the dust to see a very angry Amanda Li. "Second base takes the throw from catcher. You're supposed to back me up."

I dusted myself off. "Sorry. On the Monsters, I . . ."

"This isn't the Minors," she snapped.

No kidding.

The first couple of innings were quiet. Dad showed Kristin how to catch in the *up* position, so she wouldn't get swept away by Allie's fastballs. Rather than squatting down, Kristin bent forward at her waist with the glove arm straight out. That way she could brace herself with her upper legs. She had a few passed balls but the Hawks were scoreless after three. I had no errors because no balls were hit to me. Or to anyone else, for that matter, because no batter could touch Allie's pitching. I was right, the Blazers were boring.

I batted for the first time in the bottom of the third. Dad had prepared me before he went to the coach's box. "The Hawks' pitcher's got good control, but she's not speedy. Go for anything in the strike zone." Sounded easy to me.

The pitcher wound up and *whap!* The ball was in the catcher's mitt before I saw it. Strike one. I rubbed my eyes. Not speedy, Dad had said. So why hadn't I seen the ball?

The pitcher fired again. This time I saw the ball, coming right at my head. I jumped back so hard I stumbled. "Strike two!" the ump roared.

"It almost hit me!" I protested.

"Not really, young lady. Pitch caught the inside corner."

I dusted off my butt and stepped back in. Dad still had the hit-away on. I tensed, determined not to be fooled again. The Hawk pitcher wound up, delivered, and I swung. When I realized the ball was bouncing along the ground, it was too late. The bat was wrapped around my back.

"Strike three."

I buried myself in a corner of the dugout. Jeni patted me on the shoulder. "Nice try, Mol. You'll get her next time."

Allie just snorted.

Going into the top of the fourth, the Blazers were ahead 2–0. Allie was zinging in the strikes, but Kristin wasn't doing as well. With the lead-off batter up, she staggered backward with each pitch. Allie threw a ripping strike three, but Kristin dropped it. The batter took off for first base. Kristin just stood there while Dad, Jeni, and Allie screamed, "First! Throw to first!"

"What's going on?" I asked.

"Dropped third strike," Amanda yelled as she ran to back up first base. In Majors, the batter can steal first on a dropped third strike if the base is empty. I had forgotten that and so had Kristin; by the time she threw to Jeni, the runner was already on her way to second. Jeni whipped the ball to second base, but no one was covering and the ball bounced into the outfield. Lauren flew in to retrieve it and threw hard to home, barely missing the runner. The runner slid in under Kristin's glove, scoring the Hawks' first run. After striking out!

Dad called time and went to the mound. The infielders gathered around.

"What's going on, ladies? It looks like a circus out there."

Amanda glared at me. "Molly should have been covering second."

I protested. "You said you were covering second . . ."

"On the steal of second. On a throw to first, I back

up first. You take second." She looked disgusted, like my math teacher does when I mess up fractions.

"Okay. Molly and Kristin have to get used to their new positions," Dad said. "Let's help them out a bit. Kristin, how are you holding up?"

"I'm real tired, Mr. Burrows."

"You're doing just fine."

"I mean, like really tired." She rubbed the dirt on her face; her sweat made it muddy.

"Hang in there. A couple more innings." Dad trotted back to the bench while we went to our positions. Kristin slowly pulled on her mask.

The next batter for the Hawks was Hope Potter.

Amanda hissed at me. "She's got the highest batting average in the league." So what, I thought. Allie had already struck her out twice.

Allie brought her hands together to present the ball, swung her right arm back, forward, and whoosh, around so fast I saw only a red blur. Hope took a mighty swing and *whap!* The bat was around. Only then did the ball cross the plate.

"What the heck was that?" Hope asked the umpire.

"Strike one!" he said.

"What the heck was that?" I asked Amanda.

"Change-up."

"Huh?"

Amanda explained. "You do a fastball delivery but take all the speed off. Fool the batter."

We infielders settled into our ready positions, gloves down, weight shifting from foot to foot.

60

Allie pitched and *bam!* The ball was a blur. Hope swung but came up empty.

"Don't bother asking," Amanda said. "That was Allie's riser."

I didn't know what a riser was. Or that Allie had one. I had a lot to learn about my sister—and the game of fast-pitch softball.

Two strikes. Allie pitched and *pow!* This time Hope got a piece of it, a blazing ground ball down the middle. I cut in front of second base. I felt the ball hit my glove, so I squeezed and it stuck. Still running, I pulled it out of my glove and threw it.

Too hard.

The ball got to the base before Hope did. Unfortunately, it kept going. Over Jeni's outstretched glove. Over the fence. Into the stands. Into someone's grandmother. Good thing she had a huge purse to use as a shield.

Hope trotted to second base—one base on an overthrow to out-of-bounds.

In the dugout, Dad folded his arms over his chest and twiddled his fingers. "Fantastic stop, Mol. Just look before you throw, okay?"

Hope took a sprinter's stance at second. Amanda shot me a glance. "We're watching for a bunt. That means you move ahead of the runner to cover third."

Dad pulled Laura Ramon, the third baseman, up the line. The batter squared away in the box. Allie threw one inside. The batter swiped and missed. I took off for third, trying to get ahead of Hope, who was racing for the base. Laura hit the ground, so Kristin could make the throw down the line. The ball flew into the dirt, and Hope, sliding into my tag, knocked it out of my glove. She jumped up and ran.

I dug the ball from under my feet and whipped it to Kristin, standing right in front of the plate. It's one thing for Summer Comeau to cover the plate like that— she's big and strong—but Kristin was small. Hope went down for her slide and took Kristin with her into a pile of arms, legs, and dust. The umpire put his hands, palms down, over the whole mess. Hope was safe!

Dad called time and we gathered again at the mound.

"You okay, Kris?"

Kristin looked like she had been steamrolled. "I suppose," she said.

"Okay, girls, it's a new game. Let's get them out one-two-three and then do some damage with our bats."

My sister went to a full count on the next batter. After each pitch Kristin took her time returning the ball to Allie.

Allie was determined not to let this batter get away. She threw a smoking fastball right down the middle. Kristin stuck her glove out and the ball popped right in—and kept going. The ball and the glove sailed away and slammed against the backstop!

The confused umpire called strike three and the batter stole first and steamed toward second. Kristin just stood there staring at her gloveless left hand. Allie ran in to grab the ball. She had to shake it out of Kristin's glove and throw it to third, too late to get the runner.

Without a word, Allie handed Kristin her glove.

Kristin slammed it into the dust at home plate and walked off the field.

"Kristin?" Dad asked as she walked past him, head down.

We all watched as she walked through the parking lot and down the street. She didn't look at anyone. By the time Dad had gathered us at the pitcher's mound, Kristin was a faraway speck, heading for home.

Allie kicked at the pitcher's rubber, breaking apart chunks of clay and grinding them under her foot. Dad was grim. "I need a catcher." He looked at Jeni, Amanda, Laura. They all shook their heads no. He raised his eyebrows at Kelly, Lauren, Alyssa, Erin. More no's. He looked at Rhianna. A big chance for a bench warmer. She was quick to answer.

"No way."

He never even asked me.

Chapter Nine

Amanda finished the game as pitcher. Tossing underhand, she gave up six runs in the last two innings. Allie went to short, Rhianna got her big chance at second, Alyssa went to catcher, and I went to the bench. We lost 8–3. The Blazers' second loss in a row.

The ride home was miserable. I huddled in the back seat, the gloomy silence hanging over me like a bad report card. Mom greeted us with a big smile that fell off her face when she saw Dad and Allie with their tight mouths and dark eyes. They walked by her without a word. I followed, carrying my glove and Allie's equipment bag. Mom grabbed me.

"Molly! What are you doing in that Blazers uniform?"

"Beth couldn't be on the Blazers, so Dad drafted me up."

"Oh, he did, did he?" She looked peeved, then she

flashed me a mother's smile. You know, the kind that mothers paste on their faces when they want you to think everything is okay. "So how'd you do?" she asked, trying to sound bright and cheerful. Her voice cracked on the "do" as if she were afraid of the answer.

"Don't ask," I said and ran upstairs. I wanted to get out of the Blazer uniform and forget the whole thing.

After a quick supper of grilled cheese sandwiches, Allie and I were sent to finish our homework while Dad and Mom went over to Kristin's house. Mom told us that Dad apologized for putting her in a difficult position and thanked her for her effort. She agreed to come back and play shortstop.

Where did that leave me?

After school the next day I put on my Monsters uniform. When Dad got home I was sitting on the front step with my glove and bat, ready to go to my game. The Monsters were playing the Bombers and I wanted to get some revenge. "Mol, what are you doing?" Dad asked.

"Waiting for you to take me to the field."

Dad sat down next to me. "You're on the Blazers now."

"You don't need me on the Blazers," I said. Each word felt like a tooth being pulled, but I had to say them. "The Cookie Monsters need me."

"Mol, once a girl gets drafted up to an older league, she can't go back down for the rest of the season."

"You mean I'm stuck on the Blazers?"

"You'll do all right, honey. You need to learn a few

things, but I think you can help the Blazers out." He gave me a squeeze and went into the house. I stayed on the step for a long time.

I guess I was practicing my bench sitting.

After supper we had a family conference. "Here's the problem," Dad said. "The Blazers don't have a catcher good enough for Allie and none of the other teams will trade with us. We've got two options. One, Allie stays with the Blazers and plays infield. Amanda and Laura do some pitching and we do the best we can to finish out the season."

"What is the other option, Tom?" Mom asked quietly.

"I get calls all the time from coaches in other towns. They would love to have Allie pitching for them. We've never considered that because Brookdale has the best softball program in this part of the state. But now . . ." He looked sideways at Allie. She was staring at her hands.

"Plainville has an excellent program. Bob Kingsford has been in touch again this week, wondering if Allie would like to switch into their league."

"Is that allowed?" Mom asked.

"Allie is too good for the sport to let her flounder. I'm sure the state commissioner will help us work something out," Dad said. His voice sounded hard.

"Tom, you keep bending rules, you're going to break something," Mom replied. She sounded tired. Allie flicked her eyes up at Dad, but he didn't notice.

"I'm doing what's best for Allie."

Mom sighed. That was Dad's final line in any discussion—whatever was best for Allie. "Plainville is forty-five minutes away. How would we manage that?" Mom asked.

"I'd have to give up coaching the Blazers and make the trip with Allie every afternoon. It's a lot to think about. But the most important thing is that a pitcher of Allie's ability has to keep pitching."

Bad enough being stuck on a team that doesn't need me, but without Dad coaching, I'd never get to play. I hated Allie for messing everything up. She didn't look so special, sitting across from me at the table with her hair hanging in her face and her mouth glum. But the world, with me in it, seemed to keep revolving around her.

"Bob's offered to set up a scrimmage tomorrow night, so Allie can go pitch for his team and see how it goes. What do you think, sweetheart? Want to give it a try?"

Allie nodded a tiny yes.

I wasn't invited.

Allie and Dad set out early the next afternoon for Plainville. Mom and Chris took me to the field for the Blazers' game against the last-place team, the Firebirds. Mr. Polaski was coaching in my father's absence and had the team on the field. Kristin was back at shortstop and Rhianna was at third. Laura Ramon would be starting pitcher for the Blazers.

I trotted over to Mr. Polaski at home plate. "Where should I go?" I asked. He seemed surprised to see me;

I think he had forgotten that I was on the Blazers now.

"Molly." There was a long pause as he looked at his field. The infield was set and he already had three girls in the outfield. "Go to right field and help out."

I spent fifteen minutes watching everyone else fielding ground balls and pop flies.

When the Blazers took the field in the first inning, I was on the bench alone. Erin had taken Jeni's place at first, so Jeni could catch, Rhianna took Laura's place at third, so Laura could pitch, and Kelly was home with the chicken pox.

Laura Ramon is a great third baseman but a so-so pitcher. She used the windmill motion, but she didn't stand up straight and she released the ball way out in front, like she was bowling. The game seesawed with the Blazers pulling ahead in the top of each inning and the Firebirds catching up. Since the Firebirds usually got blown out of the park by the Blazers, their bench was screaming wild.

Mr. Polaski made some changes in the third inning. Laura went to third, Rhianna moved to second, and Amanda went to pitcher. I looked at him eagerly, hoping I would be going somewhere, but Mr. Polaski kept his nose in the score book.

After five innings the score was Blazers 12, Firebirds 8. Even without Allie the Blazers are a dynamite team.

Then disaster struck. And this time it was mine, not Allie's.

Amanda had pitched two decent innings. When the

Blazers came up to bat in the top of the sixth she laid a bombshell on Mr. Polaski.

"I've got to go now. My school's having the Science Fair tonight." Amanda goes to St. Mary's, a private school across town.

Mr. Polaski's mouth fell open. "But . . . but . . . you didn't tell me you couldn't stay for the whole game!"

"I told Mr. Burrows two weeks ago. See ya!" She grabbed her bat and glove and ran off.

Mr. Polaski rubbed his sweaty bald head with the back of his hand. He looked at the girls on the bench then at me. "Molly, go in to bat for Amanda. She's up second this inning."

I grabbed my bat and ran to the on-deck circle. I pulled on my batting gloves and began stretching my arms while I watched the pitches coming in to Laura. Pretty tame, I thought.

Laura thought so, too. She whacked one hard for a double. I stood into the batter's box and winked at my mom behind the backstop.

"Come on, Mol, I know you can do it," she urged.

The first pitch was a fat, juicy strike so I slammed it. I heard Mom yell "Go." In the coach's box, Mr. Polaski was swinging his hand in a circle, so I ran full speed around first into second. I made the turn and looked at Jeni, coaching third. She gave me the go-ahead. I hit third in a dusty slide. The crowd cheered as I stood up to enjoy my first Major League hit—a triple! Too bad Dad wasn't there to see it. But he was off to Plainville, doing what was best for Allie.

Kristin knocked me in with a nasty single to right field. We added three more runs after that and went into the bottom of the last inning with a nine-run lead.

I grabbed my glove and ran to Mr. Polaski. "Where do you want me to go?" Any position, even right field, would have made me happy after the triple I had hit.

He handed me a ball. "How about finishing off the game for us?"

"Huh?" I said.

"Pitch the last inning."

My breath left me in a big *whoosh*. The ball rolled out of my hand and bounced off my foot. Everything suddenly was hazy.

"Molly. Hurry up. You only get eight pitches for warm-ups." Mr. Polaski put the ball back in my hand and pushed me out toward the mound. I turned slowly and saw him walking away from me.

"Mr. Polaski," I called. I could feel that old worm in my stomach, making me want to throw up.

"What is it?" he asked.

"I don't pitch," I protested, holding my stomach so it wouldn't jump out of my mouth. "I don't know how."

He walked back to me and put his hand on my shoulder. "Neither does anyone else on this team," he said. "But you are Allie Burrows's sister. So go give it a try."

Chapter Ten

When I was seven my dad sent me to pitching school. After eight weeks of throwing the ball everywhere, including fifty feet straight up through the gym's ceiling, Dad agreed Allie's magic wasn't going to happen for me.

So here's all I'll say about that night and then I never want to talk about it again. I gave up ten runs in the bottom of the seventh, losing the game 18–17. I threw countless balls over the backstop. I hit four batters and I don't think I threw more than four or five strikes. The only thing good I can say about it is that I stayed on the mound to the bitter end. I was a big loser that night, but I'll never be a quitter.

It didn't help to get home and listen to Dad bragging about the Plainville Rockets. "The Plainville fields are great, well kept and even had lights for night play. Bob Kingsford is an excellent coach, knows fast-pitch inside and out. Works with the girls beautifully. The team is well trained and friendly. The catcher is rock solid. And Allie threw a one-hitter against the top team in the league, the Jets. The Rockets are dying to have her pitch for them." He finally took a breath. "By the way, how did the Blazers do?"

Mom gave me a look full of love. "Another rough night, Tom. But Molly slammed a triple and drove in a run."

"Great, Mol!" Dad said. He waited to hear more, but Mom knew just what to say.

"Molly and Allie, go to bed. We've had enough softball for one night."

I had had enough softball to last a lifetime.

The next day Allie stayed home from school. She told Mom that she had a stomachache.

After school, I was coming out of the bathroom into the upstairs hall when I heard a strange noise. It sounded like a sick kitten. I put my ear against Allie's bedroom door.

Allie was crying.

I couldn't remember ever hearing Allie cry before. Not sad crying like this. When she gets angry sometimes she bursts into tears, but she's red hot, yelling and stomping all over the place. When she's hurt, like the time she took a line drive in the knee, she goes all white and cold and the tears just freeze in her eyes. But this crying was different. In a way, it made me want to cry, too.

I knocked lightly on her door. "Allie?"

Allie opened the door a crack. "What do you want,

Mol?" she asked. She had dark patches under her eyes.

"Are you okay?"

"Yeah. Thanks for asking." She closed the door quietly. It occurred to me that Allie might be so ill that she was delirious. I could think of no other reason for her politeness. So I ran to my parents' bathroom and got the thermometer.

I tapped on the door with my fingernails. "Allie, are you asleep?"

"No."

"Allie, I think I should take your temperature."

"You don't need to."

"I think you might be sicker than Mom realizes."

Allie opened the door. I jumped back, in case she was going to push me against the wall or slam the door in my face. But she just smiled at me. Not her victory smile or her nasty smile. Just a sad smile.

"Molly, I'm not really sick." She started to close the door but I put my shoulder into it.

"What's the matter then?"

She closed her eyes slowly and I could see the dampness under her black eyelashes. The fire was gone.

"There's nothing the matter. Except I'm stuck in a place where I can't win, no matter what I do."

I left her alone. What else could I do?

Allie went to school on Thursday and Friday, but when we got home she stayed in her room. She didn't even pitch with Dad; she told him that her arm was sore.

The Blazers' next game wasn't until Monday. Dad told Allie she had to decide by Sunday whether she would stay with the Blazers or finish the season with the Plainville Rockets. She refused to talk about it.

Saturday was warm and sunny and Chris was at my door early. "Want to go on an adventure?"

Did I ever.

While I was finishing my chores, Mom packed a nice lunch for Chris and me: fat chicken sandwiches on hamburger rolls, homemade brownies, and juicy oranges.

Chris went to the garage to load up our knapsacks. I was upstairs, taking my laundry to the bathroom, when the phone rang. It was Jeni, wanting to talk to Allie. I walked the portable phone into Allie's room, where she sat in a daze—head pressed against the glass, staring out the window.

"Jeni's on the phone," I said.

She didn't even turn around. "I'll call her later."

"She'll call you later," I said into the phone, feeling silly since Allie was six feet away. "She wants to know when," I said to Allie.

"Later," was all Allie would say. I clicked off the phone and was about to return it to the hall table. But something made me stop.

"Hey, Al."

"What?"

I didn't know what. I just wanted to stop her from staring. "Chris and I are going on an adventure. Want to come?"

She had a faraway look, as if she were trying to see past the trees, past the neighborhood, maybe into last summer when she was still number one. "No thanks."

Allie was the biggest pain-in-the-butt in the world. But she was still my sister, and I knew deeper in my heart than I have ever known anything that she had to get her face away from the window.

"Allie, come with us. We had a lot of fun last week."

"I'm not interested in kids' games," she said.

"Biking and hiking and climbing are not kids' games," I said, knowing full well that what made biking and hiking and climbing so much fun were the monsters and bad guys we chased while we were doing it.

"I don't feel like it." She rolled off the chair onto her bed and stared at the ceiling.

"We climbed Mount Q last week. Did you ever climb it?" I asked.

She barely heard me. "Huh?"

"Did you ever climb Mount Q?" I persisted.

"No. Why would I want to?"

"Because . . ." I was at a loss for words. "Chris says he can climb it faster than anyone. Even you." Chris had said no such thing.

"I doubt that," she said. She rolled over and looked straight at me. But I still didn't see the fire in her eyes.

"If you don't come with us, he's going to tell everyone on the school bus you were chicken. That he's the best climber in the neighborhood. Maybe the best in town."

"So what do I care?" Allie said. "So what do I care about anything?"

My brain was stretched to the limit, trying to find a way to make Allie care about something. I heard Dad coming up the stairs. He came into Allie's room, carrying a bucket of balls and their gloves.

"Let's do some pitching," he said cheerfully. He smiled at Allie and didn't even seem to notice me.

Allie looked at Dad and then me, back to Dad, back to me.

"Not now, Dad," she said.

"Yes now."

"I'm going for a bike ride with Molly."

"Allie, you've got to have your workout," Dad said.

Allie flashed Dad a look of blue fire, and I realized then that even Dad sometimes found Allie hard to take. "I supposed we can do it when you get back," he said and walked out.

Allie stood up slowly. She looked taller and skinnier than ever, but when she reached up to get her bike helmet from a shelf, I could see those stringy muscles of steel.

"So Chris Reardon thinks he's the best mountain climber in town," she said.

"Yeah," I said.

"We'll see about that," she said, with the tiniest smile.

Chris didn't know what he was in for.

Chris was so stunned that Allie was with us that he didn't say a word as we pedaled to Camp Quannapoag. We were panting too hard to talk anyway. The ride was like a secret race—Chris would pedal hard to get in front, then Allie would catch up and get in front, pumping hard to stay there. My legs were jelly by the time we reached the camp.

"Okay," said Allie, as she flung down her bike. "Let's see who can get up the mountain first."

I couldn't even walk, let alone run up Mount Q. I stalled for time by sitting down in the grass. "Let's have lunch first."

Chris wasn't much help. "Mol, it's only ten thirty."

"Oh. Well, we can't go up the mountain until we decide who we are."

"Huh?" Allie asked, her black eyebrows arching.

"Like Geronimo. Or Robin Hood. Or dinosaur hunters." Chris knew exactly what I meant.

"Oh, for Pete's sakes," Allie snapped. "How stupid."

"It's not stupid," Chris said. "There's no adventure without risk."

"I don't get why we have to pretend we're someone else." Being Allie Burrows had been so special, she'd forgotten how to play make-believe.

"Just trust us. We know what we're doing," Chris said. "I got it! Let's play space explorers."

"Yeah, we just crash-landed on a new planet." I stood up and grabbed the knapsack. "Look, over there!" I pointed to a strange building that had the words *first aid* on it. I knew that meant *poison* in alien words. "That's where they lock up humans. And stew them in pickle juice until they're just right to eat!"

"Watch out, it's a six-headed worm!" Chris shouted.

"What the heck?" yelped Allie, lifting up her sneaker to see if she had stepped on it.

"Over there! And it's coming right at us!" Chris screamed. "Let's get out of here."

He took off at top speed, heading for the woods. Allie sprinted after him. Running was something she could understand.

Once they got into the woods, I lost sight of them. I lagged behind, carrying the backpack with all our supplies, including oxygen, laser guns, and a translator machine in case the worm wanted to talk to us instead of eat us. It wasn't until I came out of the woods and started up the rock slide that I saw Allie and Chris, side by side, near the top of the ridge.

"Ahoy there!" I yelled, thinking that since we rode in spaceships it was all right to shout ahoy. Allie kept climbing, determined to get to the top before Chris. Chris, not knowing his reputation was at stake, turned and waved to me.

And disappeared from sight.

One instant he was there, the next he was gone. Like he had fallen off the face of the earth.

"Chris!" I screamed. I dropped the knapsack and scrambled up the rock slide as fast as I could. I kept slipping and ripping open my legs, but I didn't care. I screamed "Chris!" again and this time Allie, now near the top, heard me.

As I hit the bottom of the ridge, I saw her scrambling down. Then she disappeared from sight as abruptly as Chris had. My heart beat so fast I was sure it would jump out of my mouth. "Allie!" I screamed.

For a frightening moment I wondered if the six-headed worm of our imaginations had swallowed up my best friend and my sister. Allie's head reappeared over the top of a ledge. "He's here. Hurry up!"

I hustled up the rock and swung myself over onto the ledge. I inched my way toward Allie. She was looking down into a split in the cliff face. It was about four feet wide but I don't know how deep because it led into darkness. About six feet down, sitting on a tiny ledge and covered in cobwebs and dirty leaves, was Chris.

"Hey, Mol, I found the secret hiding place of the giant worm. One problem though, I think I'd better get out of here before the worm squeezes back in and crushes me." Despite the wide smile, his eyes flicked up and down nervously at the dark stone walls around him and I knew he was scared.

"Molly," Allie whispered softly. "He's too short. He can't reach to get out. We're going to have to go get help."

We both leaned back over the edge. "Chris," Allie said. "Molly's going to stay here with you and I'm going to ride home and get the police."

"No!" he bellowed, his voice echoing through the crevice. I ducked, expecting bats or hornets to come flying out of the darkness.

"Why not?" asked Allie. "You can't stay there until you grow tall enough to climb out."

"They'll laugh at me." Chris's voice cracked. He was close to tears.

"Who'll laugh at you?" I asked.

"Everyone. They'll come rescue me and they'll put

it in the newspaper and everyone will think it's funny and cute that I had to be saved because I was too short to save myself."

"That's stupid," I said.

"No it's not!" Allie snapped.

"It's not?" I asked. I was shocked to hear my sister agreeing with Chris Reardon for the first time in two years.

"No one likes to be made a fool of in public," Allie said.

"That's right," Chris said from under us.

"So what're we going to do?" I asked.

Allie lay down on her belly and reached her long arms toward Chris. "Stand up carefully and see if you can touch my fingers. Go slow." He raised himself up, balancing on the little ridge. Below him were sharp rocks and darkness.

"I can just touch," he said, panting with the effort.

"Good." Allie inched forward. "Molly, come here and sit on my legs." I crept over and did as she said, hoping I wouldn't break anything. I would punch anyone who dared to call me chubby, but I have to admit this—I was sturdy and Allie's long legs were skinny.

She reached down farther into the crevice. "Chris, grab my wrists." I couldn't see what was happening. I just sat on Allie's legs and prayed she didn't remember that time last summer when Chris filled her sneakers with tadpoles.

I heard Chris's voice from far away. "Now what?"

"Hold on tight and start climbing with your feet." I

80

realized what Allie was doing. It was the game I liked to play with Chris's baby brother, Timmy. He would hold my hands and walk up my legs, getting his whole body straight away from mine until he flipped over backward and landed on his feet. Allie's plan made sense—as long as Chris didn't flip over and tumble back into the crevice.

As Chris inched his way up toward Allie, I could see his head, then his face, then his body. He was near the top and sticking almost straight out. Allie's arms were all that kept him from the darkness.

"Now what?" he asked, his voice rattling in his throat. He was gasping and his face was red and sweaty. I looked at his hands and Allie's; they were locked at the wrists.

"Molly, slide down and grab me around the waist and get ready to pull backward." I wrapped my arms around her and planted my knees on either side of her.

"Chris, bend your knees slowly and when I say go, you jump toward me. Molly, you pull back as hard as you can." As Chris bent his legs, I could hear his sneakers slipping on the stone.

"*Go!*" Allie yelled and I yanked hard. She came flying back on top of me with Chris tumbling after her. We tangled in a pile and then I could feel us slipping toward the edge. I reached out and found a small bush growing out of the rock. I grasped it for dear life with one hand and held Allie with the other while she held Chris. After a moment we stopped slipping.

"Chris, get up carefully," Allie said. He slowly

climbed over us to safety. Allie brushed herself off and helped me up. "Good thing you're strong, Mol," she said. "You probably saved all of us."

We went to the top of Mount Q and sat for the longest time, letting the warm breeze and the bright sun wash away all of our fright. No one said anything, but we sat peacefully together, like three friends can.

I knew I was only at the top of Brookdale but I felt like I was on top of the world.

Chapter Eleven

We spent the afternoon killing space worms and blasting asteroids. When we got back home, we didn't say a word about what happened to our parents or even to each other. After supper Chris brought over some homemade cupcakes and he, Allie, and I sat on the back porch and ate them.

On Sunday afternoon Allie and I took our bikes out to the wayback yard. Allie and I carved a trail through a big pile of stone dust, so we could have a bike-jumping contest as soon as Chris returned from his grandparents' house.

Even with all the fun we were having, I couldn't forget about tomorrow night. The Blazers were supposed to play the Thunder. Would Allie play? Would I?

"What are you going to do about the game?" I asked.

"I don't know," she said. She dug a large rock out of the trail and flung it into the woods.

I raked a nest of leaves and sticks from the base of the bike jump. "Remember how you said you were in a place that no matter what you did, you were going to lose?"

"Yeah."

"What did you mean by that?"

Allie leaned on her shovel. "If I go to Plainville to play, I can pitch. But I don't know anyone there and even though the girls are nice, they'll never be my friends. How can they be if I show up a few minutes before the game and leave right afterward? And imagine how their pitcher is going to feel if I come from miles away and take her job?"

I had never thought of it that way. "That stinks."

"Yeah, but if I stay with the Blazers I can't pitch because all my friends are afraid that I'll hurt them. Since we don't have another pitcher, we don't have much of a chance of winning and everyone will blame me."

I kicked at the dirt with my heels. "I know how you feel."

"You do?"

"Yeah. I can't go back to the Monsters because it's against league rules. If I stay with the Blazers, I'm not going to play because the only position I know how to play is shortstop and Kristin is the best shortstop in the state. I might as well stay home for the rest of the season."

"It rots," Allie said.

"No kidding," I agreed.

"Oh, great," Allie said in a tone that was anything but great. "Here comes Dad."

Dad strolled across the back lawn, carrying his catcher's mitt, Allie's glove, and a bucket of balls. "How about doing some pitching, Allie?"

Allie pounded the stone dust with the shovel. "Not now," she said.

"When, Allie? You can't just give up pitching because we've hit a rough spot in the season."

"Rough spot?" she snarled. "It's more than just a rough spot."

"Allie, it's not the end of the world."

"Yes it is," she said. "And it's all your fault." She threw the shovel down, grabbed her bike, and raced away.

I just stood there, too shocked to move.

"She really didn't mean that." Dad sounded like he wanted to cry. I felt my skin go hot. I knew I was turning red. But I wasn't embarrassed. I could feel anger bubbling up from some place deep inside me, bubbling up like lava in a volcano until I exploded.

"Yes she did. It *is* your fault," I yelled.

"I suppose it is," Dad muttered. "I should have had a reserve catcher. That was stupid of me." He stared through the woods as if he could see Allie pedaling away.

I was sick and tired of Dad always looking after Allie

and ignoring me. I yanked his arm hard and turned him toward me. "That's not what I mean," I said. "It's your fault because you don't care about Allie. You said so yourself. All you care about is her fastball."

"That's not true, Molly."

"Yes it is," I said. I could feel the hot tears running down my face. "You only love Allie because she's a star pitcher. And I can't pitch or do anything that makes you proud. So you don't love me at all."

I jumped on my bike.

"Molly," Dad called. "Come back here."

I sped away as fast as I could.

"Please, Mol," he called after me.

No way, I thought. No way.

That anger that had come up from deep inside me brought with it a terrible fear. It had been there for some time now, but I had kept it hidden away. Hadn't dared think about it or even consider it. Certainly wouldn't say it out loud. But I knew it had to be true. I pedaled hard, but I couldn't escape that awful truth. My father didn't love me.

My legs were burning with pain as I flew through the backwoods, into the next neighborhood. My heart burned with a pain just as hot. Dad had the daughter he wanted, the great Allison Burrows. He didn't need me.

I made it through the backwoods and to the school before Dad caught up to me. He jumped out of the Bronco and ran across the playground.

I ran away from him, around the back of the school, through the basketball court, across the parking lot.

"Molly," he called.

"No," I yelled back. "No."

Then he caught me. "Molly," he panted. "My Molly." He picked me up and my legs and heart just hurt too much to try to get away. He wrapped his arms around me and hugged me. He held me to his chest and put his face in my hair. I could feel wet on my neck and I thought he must be sweaty. Then I realized he was crying. Crying for me.

"Daddy," I said and hugged him back. Then I cried for him.

"I'm a jerk," he said. And that's all he had to say because I knew he was a jerk, sometimes, but I also knew he did love me after all. What else mattered?

He slid me down to the ground but kept his arm around me. I grabbed his T-shirt and wiped my face, then pushed it up and wiped his face. We started to laugh and then he picked me up again. "I love you," he said. "Another thing I took for granted, that you knew that I loved you. But how could you when I don't show you?" He squeezed me tight. "I'm so sorry."

I squeezed him back. "I think I know where Allie is," I whispered.

"Let's go find her," he whispered back.

We caught up to Allie before she reached the top of Mount Q. I was just as glad—I don't think any of us had the energy to make it to the top. The three of us climbed onto a boulder. Dad sat between us and put his arms around us. "I need to apologize to both of you. I really messed up."

"No kidding," Allie said.

"Allie, I put too much pressure on you. And Molly, I ignored you. You both deserved better from me. I was too busy trying to be a super coach to be a good father. I screwed up both jobs."

"Dad, it's not the end of the world," Allie said. I couldn't help myself—I laughed.

"Let's make it the beginning," Dad said with a smile. "If you'll forgive me."

I squeezed him hard while Allie slipped her arm around him. We sat there for a long time, watching the May breeze dance in the trees below us. Then Dad got up and stretched his legs.

"Enough sitting. How about we get some ice cream?" he asked.

Allie looked at me like she had something on her mind. "Can we go after supper, Dad?"

"Sure."

"Molly and I will ride our bikes home. Okay?"

"If that's what you want," he said.

Allie looked at me again. "Yeah," I said. When we got back to the camp he unloaded my bike from the Bronco. Then he bent down and kissed me. "I love you, Molly."

"Love you, too," I whispered.

Dad reached over and rubbed Allie's hair and then got in the car and drove off.

"So what's up?" I asked Allie.

"I'm a jerk, too," she said.

No kidding, I almost said out of habit. But I didn't because I knew she wasn't a jerk.

"Nah," I said.

"I'm a good pitcher and a rotten sister," she said.

"No you're not," I said again. "You're a great pitcher and a not-so-bad sister."

We both laughed and hopped on our bikes. On the way home we rode by the ball park. I turned in and Allie followed me.

"What are you doing?" she asked. "We've got to get home for supper."

"Wait a minute, Allie." I stood in the infield and closed my eyes. The park was deserted, but I could imagine the noise of the crowd and the smell of the hamburgers and the crack of the bat. I imagined Allie on the mound, throwing balls so fast I could barely see them. I could see tall Jeni at first, stretching in the dirt to snag throws and get runners out. And Lauren in center, running, running, running until she snatched a fly ball out of the air. There was Dad cheering Rhianna on, making her feel like she was the best hitter in California even though she struck out every time.

"Hey, Al?"

"What?" said Allie. She was in her own daydream, staring at home plate.

"I'll make you a deal. I'll stay with the Blazers if you do."

She smiled. Not a victory smile or a nasty smile or a

sad smile. A real smile that a friend gives to another friend.

"Deal," she said. "We'll tell Dad tonight. After he buys us the biggest ice cream cones ever."

Chapter Twelve

Dad called Mr. Kingsford to let him know that Allie would stay in Brookdale. Then he phoned Mr. Polaski. "We won't even worry about playoffs," Dad said. "Let's just have some fun."

On Monday the Blazers were scheduled to play the Thunder. When we got to the field, Dad posted the new lineup:

Kristin	SS	SUBS
Laura	3B	Rhianna
Jeni	1B	Molly
Allie	2B	
Lauren	CF	
Kelly	C	
Amanda	P	
Alyssa	LF	
Erin	RF	

Everyone ran to their positions for warm-ups. Allie sparkled at second base and Amanda kept looking back at her from the pitcher's mound. I think she was nervous about losing her position.

During fielding practice, Dad sent me to double up behind Laura at third. Laura stepped aside and let me take my first grounder. I scooped the ball easily, but as I stretched to throw to first I realized the base was in the wrong place. Well, that's not exactly right. *I* was in the wrong place—third base—when I was used to making the throw to first base from shortstop. I threw the ball way over Jeni's glove, over the fence, and into the stands. Which were still empty, thank heavens.

I waited for Dad or Jeni or Laura to yell at me. Instead Dad tossed me another ball. "Look at Jeni. Learn the range. Then throw." I threw right on target. Dad hit me a scorcher. I scooped it and threw it to Jeni, this time right in her glove. She didn't even have to stretch.

"Nice work, Mol," he said.

"Good play," said Laura. "You'll take my job away."

Even Amanda turned and winked.

The Blazers were visitors that night. Normally, you want to be home team, so you can have last ups in the game. But with weak pitching, Dad was happy to have his team bat first. He said he wanted to gain a psychological advantage. In other words, he wanted the Blazers to pound out a big lead and make the Thunder play catch-up.

Kristin led off with a deep infield single. On the next pitch, she was down to second like a flash. Laura bunted her to third. Jeni laced a single into left field, sending Kristin home and Laura to third. Allie was up.

"Hey, let's cheer," I said. Everyone on the bench looked at me like I was wacky.

"We are cheering," said Amanda. "Come on Allie, hit one."

"I mean real cheers. Like ducks on the pond."

"We used to do that in Minors," Kelly said. "How come we don't do those anymore?"

"We've outgrown that," Amanda said.

"Never," I said and started it.

> There's two ducks on the pond,
> Want another one on.
> Get a hit quack, quack,
> Get a hit!

Allie slammed a double, clearing the bases. She quacked at us from second. Lauren came up and Erin decided to try one: "Hit till you puke."

Even I looked at her like she was nuts.

"Come on, Mol. Cheer."

She screamed:

> Hit till you
> Hit till you
> Hit till you

And I screamed back: "puke."

Lauren hit a double, sending Allie home. Kelly called over from the on-deck circle. "I don't want to puke. But I do want some cheers."

Allie came and sat next to me. I high-fived her for her

double. She began a cheer that I didn't know, but Laura and Kristin, who had played Minors with Allie, remembered:

Allie:	When I say go, you say . . .
Rest:	Fight.
Allie:	When I say win, you say . . .
Rest:	Tonight.
Allie:	When I say boogie, you say. . . .
Rest:	Down.
Allie:	When I say all, you say . . .
Rest:	Right.
Everyone:	Go fight,
	Win tonight.
	Boogie down,
	All right, all right.

When the Blazers took the field in the bottom of the first, we had a nine-run lead with the Thunder coming to bat. Amanda took the mound and threw a lot of strikes. Dad taught her how to pull her arm back, then snap the ball at her hip so it came in fast. He called it modified fast-pitch. Not the same as the full windmill motion but effective. The Thunder did some hitting, but the Blazers kept the runs down. Rhianna and I kept the cheering going from the bench. We yelled "Three up, three down" every time the Blazers took to the field.

At the end of the game, the Blazers had the win. It wasn't pretty, with a score of 24 to 13, but it was a win just the same. I played two innings at third and Rhianna played half the game in the outfield. Rhianna almost got a hit, but she was thrown out at first. I had a wicked sore throat from cheering, but I didn't care. Dad invited the whole team to get ice cream, and Kelly and Rhianna raced to Dad's Bronco, so they could ride with me.

Just as we were pulling out, Amanda banged on the passenger-side window. Dad opened the door and she squeezed in next to me.

"How come you guys didn't wait for me?" she said. "Hey, Mr. Burrows, do you mind if we do some cheers?"

Dad didn't mind at all.

We were having so much fun that the end of the season came before we knew it. Every night that we didn't have a game, Dad, Allie, Chris, and I went to our back-yard and played ball. Mom played outfield. Sometimes we played baseball, sometimes softball. Jeni and Kristin came over one night and we played football. It was Allie, Chris, and I versus Dad, Jeni, and Kristin, with Mom as permanent center. I was quarterback and Allie was my wide receiver. We won.

Every weekend we went adventuring. Our gang of adventurers grew as Amanda and Erin joined us as well as Eric and Jonathan, two of Chris's friends. We fought gangsters in the school yard, pirates at Lake Quannapoag, and nasty aliens on invisible motorcycles that dared to invade our bike track.

In the last week of the season, Dad gave everyone on the Blazers a chance to play any position they wanted. Rhianna tried to pitch. She wasn't much better than I was, but she tried so hard that Dad promised to get her into a pitching school next winter. I played center field, a position that worked out great because try as I might, when I threw the ball to home, I couldn't throw it out of the park.

We won a few games. We lost some, too. Which is why when the season ended, we were all in for a surprise.

The Blazers were still in first place.

But we weren't there alone. The Sting had caught up with us. Mr. Boucher and Mr. Polaski came to see Dad about the tie. Allie and I sat in the kitchen and since no one told us to leave, we listened in.

"Tom," said Mr. Boucher. "We've got to solve this first place issue by this weekend. Regional Championships start on Monday and Brookdale has to send either the Blazers or the Sting to compete."

"Harry, I already told you. We're in no position to compete in Regionals. Send the Sting. They've earned it."

Mr. Boucher glanced sideways at Mr. Polaski. "It's not just your decision to make, Tom."

Dad glanced at Mr. Polaski, back at Mr. Boucher, back to Mr. Polaski again. I was getting dizzy watching him.

"I'm sorry, Jerry," Dad said. "I didn't intend to make the decision for both of us."

"Normally we'd have a play-off game to determine first place," said Mr. Polaski.

"We don't have a rat's chance of winning," Dad said.
"I agree."

"Then why should we put the girls through it?"

Mr. Polaski leaned over the table. "Because it's their game, not ours. If they're willing to play, we should let them."

Dad grinned at Mr. Polaski, but I could tell his heart wasn't in it. "I'll call the girls tonight. Day after tomorrow, six P.M.?"

"Yeah. I'll arrange for the umpires and scorekeeper," Mr. Boucher volunteered.

Allie wandered off to the family room, but I followed the men to the door. As Mr. Polaski was walking down the sidewalk, Dad pulled Mr. Boucher back.

"Harry, do me a favor please. For Allie's sake, let's keep the game quiet. No newspapers or TV?"

Mr. Boucher nodded and walked off to his car. Dad stood on the sidewalk staring into the night. I went out to stand with him, so he wouldn't be alone. As we looked into the bright, starry sky I knew we were thinking the same thing. Back on Opening Day in April all the newspapers and the television stations came to watch the Blazers play. To see Allie, the best fast-pitch softball pitcher in California. And here we were in June, ending the season with a sudden-death play-off, hoping no one would show up.

Our world had gotten very small.

Chapter Thirteen

As soon as we got home from school on play-off day, I got into my uniform. Allie thought I was crazy. "What are you doing? The game is three hours away."

"I don't care," I said. "This might be the last time that I'll get to wear my Blazers uniform."

"What are you talking about?"

"Next year you'll be thirteen, so you'll be playing in Seniors. So you won't be on the Blazers, so Dad won't coach them, so who knows what team I'll be on."

"I get the picture, Mol."

"Speaking of pictures—can you get dressed, so we can have our pictures taken together?"

Allie sighed. Then she flipped my hat off and said, "All right. I'll get changed."

Chris came over with his Polaroid. Allie shoved Dad's Blazers hat on Chris's head and we took pictures everywhere—on our front porch, on the backyard softball field, on the bike track. We saved the last two for family pictures, and when Dad and Mom got home from work we dragged them onto the front porch. We had one big family hug and though Chris didn't quite center us in the picture and Mom had a funny look on her face and Allie's braces reflected sunlight, it is still my favorite photo of all time.

"Girls, come on in for a quick bite before the game," Mom said.

Allie didn't have to be asked twice. I wasn't interested. "No thanks, Mom. I already had a big bowl of cereal." I said that so she wouldn't worry about me not getting my nutrition.

Why do people say they have butterflies in their stomach when they're nervous? Mine was full of buzzing bees. That beat the worm that used to live there, but it still was a nuisance. I don't know why I was frightened. It was a sudden-death play-off game and I was a bench warmer, so I didn't even expect to play. While the rest of the family ate, I hung out with Chris until it was time to leave for the field.

"So what do you want to do?" Chris asked. "Not enough time for an adventure."

"I don't care. Anything," I said.

"Hey, want to catch for me? I could use the practice." Chris was slated to be starting pitcher for his All-Star baseball game.

"Sure." I got my glove and squatted in the catcher's crouch. Chris's fastballs were whizzing, and I had to pay close attention, so I wouldn't catch one in my teeth. I didn't know Allie had come outside until she screamed at the top of her lungs.

"Molly! Molly!"

I whipped around and nearly got crowned. A rising fastball brushed the back of my head.

"Allie, what the heck?" I shouted.

She disappeared into the back of the Bronco, then reappeared with her glove and an armful of softballs. She ran over to Chris and pushed him out of the way.

"Hey, what do you think you're doing!" he yelled and then suddenly shut up. We both realized what Allie was up to.

She was going to pitch to me.

The best pitcher in California—the twelve-year-old who had terrorized her championship teammates—the girl who had a fastball like a bullet and a curve that jumped quicker than a cricket—the famous Allison Burrows—was going to pitch to me. Me, Molly Burrows—a Blazer bench warmer.

And dumb old me just squatted down and waited for her to put a ball through my head.

She presented, swung back, windmilled, and *bam!* The ball was in my face.

And in my glove!

And my hand hadn't fallen off. I shook it to make sure. It stung but it was still attached to my arm. So, dumb old me, I threw the ball back to her and let her do it again. *Bam, bam, bam!* Those scary fastballs kept sticking in my glove.

After about ten pitches, Allie started screaming again. She pitched and screamed at the same time. *Bam! Dad! Mom! Bam! Get out here! Bam! Now! Hurry! Bam!*

I didn't dare take my eyes off Allie. Chris told me later that Dad and Mom ran out of the house in a panic, Mom with the first-aid kit in her hand. They jumped down the steps just in time to see me catch one of Allie's fastballs. Mom sat down as if she were about to faint. Dad's jaw dropped. Then he yelled, too. *"Molly! Molly! Look at Molly!"*

Allie screamed with him: *"Look at Molly! Look at Molly!"*

Mom's crystal voice cut through the noise. "Allison. Thomas. Stop it. *Now.* You're making a spectacle of yourselves."

Allison and Thomas, that is, Allie and Dad, stopped. They just stared at me.

"Molly," Dad said quietly. "How about you try some catching tonight?"

I gasped. Dad smiled. "Only if you want to, Mol, only if you want to." Mom shrugged, then winked at me. Chris gave me a thumbs-up. Allie had that old fire back in her eyes.

"Sure, why not," I said.

If I were going to risk my life, at least it was for a good cause.

Chapter Fourteen

"Are you crazy?" Amanda shrieked. "She's going to kill you!"

The rest of the Blazers crowded at the dugout door, staring at the lineup:

Kristin	SS	SUBS
Laura	3B	Kelly
Jeni	1B	Rhianna
Allie	P	
Lauren	CF	
Erin	RF	
Amanda	2B	
Alyssa	LF	
Molly	C	

Laura bounded three feet in the air. "Yes! I don't have to pitch tonight!" She lowered her voice. "Poor Molly."

Erin jumped even higher. "All right! I don't have to

catch!" She hurried out to right field without even looking at me.

Rhianna wrapped her arms around me. "It was nice
knowing you," she sobbed, then dashed away.

"We're going to have to sweep you up from behind
the backstop and put you in the bat bag, so your parents can take you home!" Laura yelled, then stomped
off to the outfield.

Jeni put her hand on my shoulder. "You're a brave
woman, Molly. Good luck." She walked off to first base.

Kristin slapped me on the back as she trotted by.
"You're gonna need it. Man, are you gonna need it."

Dad and I were alone on the bench. "I've got to
warm up Allie," he said. "You get the catcher's equipment on."

"All by myself?" I gulped.

Dad laughed. "No. Not all by yourself." He winked
over my head. I turned and saw Mick Pimental standing behind me.

"Well, young lady," Mick said gruffly. "Why didn't
you tell me you were a catcher?"

"I didn't know I was," I said, and Mick and Dad
laughed.

"She's all yours," Dad said. He reached out and
shook Mick's hand. "Thanks for the help," he said and
went off to warm Allie up. Mr. Polaski was giving the
rest of the team fielding practice. I looked up at Mick.

"Well, get your gear on, Molly," he said. I dumped
the catcher's equipment and let it sit in a pile of dirt. I
didn't know where to begin. I picked up a shin pad and
buckled it around my leg.

"The buckles go on the outside, Mol. Here, let me show you how to loosen the straps." I handed them over and he adjusted the straps.

"Let's do the helmet and mask next," he said. "You want to make sure the mask is tight enough to protect your face but with enough give in it so you can whip it off."

"Whip it off?" I asked.

"Yeah, when you go after foul balls. You have to get the helmet off, so you can look up."

I had forgotten how much there was to catching. Going after fouls and bunts. Throwing runners out at second and third. Making the play at home. It was almost too much to think about.

"Molly." Mick shook my arm gently. "I'll be sitting right behind the backstop. I'll be with you on every play. You don't have to worry about anything."

The bees in my stomach stopped buzzing. Mick fastened the chest protector around me and I stood up, ready to go into battle against the Sting.

"Wait a minute, Mol. Your sister throws some fire. You'd better use this." He fished a foam glove out of his pocket. "Put this on under your glove. Remember to try to catch the ball in the pocket. And whatever you do, keep your throwing hand behind your back."

"Behind my back?"

"You don't want Allie to break all your fingers, do you?"

The bees started to buzz again, but I rubbed my tummy and made them go away. The only thing I would let Allie break that night was the tie for first place.

Jeni and Lauren joined the umpire and the two Sting captains at home plate for the coin toss. The Blazers lost, which meant the Sting would be home team and we would have first ups.

As Kristin and Laura got ready to bat in the number one and two spots, Dad studied Meghan King warming up. Mr. Polaski took off his hat and scratched his balding head.

"She's not as good as Allie," he said.

"Maybe not. But she's very good. And Allie hasn't pitched for a month. It's going to be an interesting game, Jerry."

Mr. Polaski glanced my way. "I'll say."

Dad gave Kristin and Laura some last-minute instructions, then trotted to the first-base coaching box. Mr. Polaski, scorebook in hand, took charge of the dugout.

The umpire yelled, "Play ball!"

And did we ever.

Meghan was hot and sat Kristin, Laura, and Jeni down 1–2–3 in the first inning. Too soon it was our turn to take the field. I went to catcher and Mick came with me.

Countless players had worn two foot holes about three feet behind the plate. "Here's where you crouch down, Mol. You hold your glove out like this," he said, showing me how to extend my arm halfway. "Never get any closer than this to the batter."

"How come?"

"If your glove touches the batter or crosses over the plate you'll get called for interference. But even more

105

important, if you're too close a batter could slam your hand with her bat. We wouldn't want that to happen."

I began to wonder if there were enough catcher's equipment in the world to keep me safe.

I squatted down, so Allie could warm up. She started slow, then blasted the last few pitches. Just like in Chris's front yard, my glove seemed to know where to go to catch the ball. Dad nodded as each pitch came in with a *slap* or a *pop*.

The ump said, "Last one." That meant I had to throw my practice ball to second base after the next pitch. When the catcher does that it's called "coming down" because the ball's coming down from home to second to catch an imaginary runner stealing from first base. I held my breath, whipped the ball to second, and didn't breathe until I saw the ball sitting tightly in Amanda's glove.

"Nice throw," Allie called.

"Batter up," the umpire barked.

When the first batter stepped up, Mick hissed at me from behind the backstop. "Call the play, Mol."

I shouted, "No outs, play's at first!"

Amanda, positioned between first and second base, starting laughing. "No kidding, Molly."

Allie turned sharply and Amanda froze. Allie turned back to me and smiled. The batter stepped in, I put my glove up, and *whoosh!* Allie delivered her first pitch. Right into the glove, strike one. The next two were in there for strikes two and three and we had one out. Only seventeen more batters and I could go home.

The second batter was retired with a weak pop-up

to Laura at third. After the play, Mick reminded me, "Mol, take your mask off for plays like that."

Allie got two quick strikes on the third batter, followed by two balls. With the count two and two, the batter tipped the next pitch up in the air to the back of home plate. I whipped off the helmet and peered up for the ball. I heard footsteps coming at me. Jeni was rushing in from first base. I saw the ball almost above me, a bit to my right, so I yelled out, "I got it!" Eyes on the ball, glove in the air, I took a couple of steps.

And fell. Right on my face. The ball thudded next to me and rolled harmlessly to the fence.

I hoisted myself up to see what I had tripped over. The catcher's helmet. I looked through the fence at Mick. "My fault, Molly," he said. "After you take it off, fling it in the opposite direction of the ball."

Now he tells me.

I pulled the mask and helmet back on and squatted down. Allie boomed in a low, fast one. The batter swung and the bat moving across the plate distracted me. I fumbled the ball, then dropped it at my feet. The umpire bellowed, "Strike three." The batter bolted for first. "First base!" screamed Allie.

I dug the ball out of the dirt and flung it to first. Except it didn't go to first. It sailed beyond the base into right field. Erin was on her toes and snatched the ball before the runner dared to take second. I opened my mouth to apologize to Allie, but she cut me off. "It's okay, Mol. Leave her to me." She winked at me and scowled at the Sting's cleanup hitter.

Allie scooped up a handful of dirt. She ground it to

powder in her right hand, then tossed it aside. She presented, swung back and . . .

Nothing. What happened to the pitch?

Allie swung around to first and fired the ball to Jeni. The runner was caught off the base and Jeni tagged her for the third out. Allie grinned at me. "See. I told you I'd take care of it."

Allie held the Sting hitless for four innings. They had an occasional base runner—I dropped some balls, booted one to third base, and let a few pass by. In the fifth, Allie lost steam and gave up a single and then a double. The Sting scored a run before she shut them down for the inning. The Blazers went into the sixth inning behind 1–0. If we didn't score, the game was over.

As we got ready to bat, Dad huddled with Mr. Polaski. "Put Rhianna in to pinch-hit for Alyssa," Dad said.

Mr. Polaski winced. "Tom, she's only had one hit all season."

Dad pushed his cap back on his head. "Let's give her a chance to surprise us."

Mr. Polaski walked into the dugout. "Come on Blazers, get some runs. Erin's up with Amanda on deck. Rhianna, you'll be after Amanda, batting for Alyssa. Molly, you'll be hitting fourth."

"Molly, I'm gonna strike out!" Rhianna clutched my arm. "I'm gonna make the last out in the game. I could just die."

I had to calm her down before she broke my arm. "Hey, I'm still alive." I wiggled my ears to convince her.

108

"You thought Allie was going to kill me. And she hasn't. Right?"

Rhianna examined me carefully. "Right."

"My dad wouldn't put me behind the plate if he thought I was going to get hurt or do something stupid, right?"

"I suppose."

"Well he wouldn't put you in to hit if he thought you would get hurt or do something stupid. He's counting on you," I said.

"He is?" She stood up slowly, not quite convinced.

"You bet." I handed her a helmet. "You can do it!"

"Yeah, I can do it," she said, with a spring in her step. On her way to the on-deck circle she passed Amanda, who had just struck out. Rhianna glanced back at me and I gave her a thumbs-up.

As Rhianna watched Meghan blazing balls by Erin, I could see her lips moving: *I can do it, I can do it.*

Erin flied to right field for the second out and it was Rhianna's turn. I went to the on-deck circle. If Rhianna could do it like I promised she could, then I would have to do it, too.

If I didn't, I would kill our chances for the championship.

I chanted to myself: *I can do it, I can do it.*

Chapter Fifteen

Before Rhianna stepped in for the first pitch, the Sting catcher called time. A strap on her helmet had broken and needed to be repaired. Rhianna stiffened as if she was in a giant freezer. Dad went to talk to her during the time-out.

Would it be better for Rhianna to get on and let me get the last out? Or should she make the last out and save me from having to do it? While I was trying to figure this out, Mick came to the fence.

"You're looking good, Mol."

"Thanks," I said. "Can I ask you something, Mr. Pimental?"

"Sure," he said.

"Why are you doing this? Helping me, I mean?"

"Why do you ask?"

"Well," I said. "You coached the Sting for years. You know most of the girls on the team. So why help me? I'm on the other team and my dad—well, you and my dad—"

"Your father and I aren't exactly best friends."

"Nope," I said.

"I started this season with you and I'm going to finish it with you. That simple."

"Oh," I said. It felt good to have all these people—Mick, Dad, Allie—believing in me.

"So what do you think of Meghan King?" he asked.

"Too fast for me," I said.

"I don't think so," he said.

"I struck out twice already!" I said. "I can't hit her."

"Yes you can," he said.

"How?"

"You know how fast Allie pitches?"

"Real fast," I said.

He smiled. "And your glove knows right where to go to catch those fast pitches, right? Without you thinking about it?"

"There's no time to think about it."

"You have what we call an *eye*."

"I have two eyes, Mr. Pimental."

He laughed. "I mean your eye knows how to see the ball. Without anyone teaching it. In fact, an eye like yours can't be taught."

"Yeah, okay." I glanced back at the field. The Sting coach was still fiddling with his catcher's helmet and Dad had Rhianna almost all thawed out.

"What I'm trying to tell you, Molly, is that if you can see the ball to catch it, you can also see the ball to hit it."

"Meghan's too fast," I protested. "I don't know when or where to swing."

"Your brain doesn't know," Mick agreed. "But your eyes and your hands do. Trust them. Can you do that?"

I nodded, knowing that I wouldn't have to do anything unless Rhianna did something first. Mick winked at me and took a package of gum out of his pocket. "Want some?"

"No, thanks."

"Neither do I, but it beats chewing that old cigar, wouldn't you say?"

Before I dared answer, the ump yelled, "Play ball!" and Rhianna stepped into the batter's box.

As Rhianna pulled the bat back and readied herself for Meghan's first pitch, I could see her lips moving: *I can do it. I can do it.*

It was Meghan who did it. She hit Rhianna right on the shoulder. Rhianna fell backward, and Dad and Mr. Polaski dashed over to her. Dad tried to get her to sit down with an ice pack, but she shook him off. She had earned first base and she was going to take it.

Which left me to make the last out.

I dusted my hands, knocked at my cleats, and gave my bat a few practice swings. Behind the backstop Mom was mumbling her "Please don't let her strike out" prayer. Chris gave me the thumbs-up. Finally the umpire scolded me. "Let's go, young lady."

I glanced down at the coaches' box. Hit away. Yeah, right, Dad.

The first pitch came flying in and I reached for it,

missing by a mile. The next one was exactly the same and I froze, bat stuck to my shoulder. Two terribly quick strikes. I stepped out and banged my cleats. The ump growled at me, so I stepped back in. Mick growled, too. "Trust your eye."

I blanked out Dad and Meghan and the Sting. I willed away the Blazers and the fans and my fear of doing something stupid. All that was left was the ball and my bat. When the ball came in, it was big and round and white and just where I wanted it. I swung my bat like a hammer, crashing into the ball to send it flying away from me, flying away from everyone.

When I came back to the world I was running for first. I could see Dad watching the ball fly, fly, fly while he was swinging his hands over his head, motioning for me to go, go, go. As I turned first I could see the ball, coming down, going over the fence in center field. Over, over, over.

Almost.

The Sting center fielder backed against the fence and jumped. The ball hit her glove, pulling her arm over the fence. She pulled her arm back into the park, bringing with her the ball.

And the third out.

The crowd cheered wildly for the spectacular catch. I trudged back from second, squeezing my eyes shut to hold back the tears. Suddenly I was lifted in the air and spun around. I felt my father's cheek against mine as he hugged me tight. "You are incredible, Molly. Just incredible."

I held on to his neck, hiding my tears in his shoulder. "I made the last out," I cried.

"Are you kidding? Yeah, the center fielder made an incredible play. But you still hit the ball out of the park against one terrific pitcher. When I'm an old, old man I'll always remember how you blasted that ball!"

And I suddenly felt like a champion.

The Sting won the game, the Brookdale championship, and a trip to the Regional playoffs.

There were no tears on the Blazers' bench. We had all done the best we could. When we congratulated the Sting there was a lot of laughing and back slapping and even some hugs. Allie and Meghan talked for a long time. Then Allie came up to me and patted my shoulder. "Good job, Mol." She patted my shoulder again. Then she hugged me.

"Aren't you upset that we lost?"

"Naw. Right now, the Sting is the best team in Brookdale. But there's always next year."

"But you're moving up to the fourteen-and-unders."

"I'll make sure Dad takes you with us."

"I'll only be eleven," I said.

"You're plenty good enough. That is, if you're interested in catching for me."

Of course I was interested. Catching for Allie Burrows was the greatest adventure of all.

Except for the one that Dad announced after he gathered us back on the bench. "Last year, when you won the State Championship, I was very proud. But today I'm even prouder than I was a year ago."

"You are?" asked Amanda.

"You bet." Dad grinned.

"How come?"

"Today you lost. But you did it like champions. You didn't grumble or blame each other. And most importantly, when you congratulated the winners, you meant it. It takes a true champion to do that. I am proud of this team and grateful to be your coach."

He turned his head away for a moment. Maybe he was even crying a little. He looked back at us and pulled something from his back pocket.

"As you know, the Sting will be going to the Regionals on Monday and if they do well, they may make it to the State Championships the week after. Meanwhile, our season is over, unless . . ." He stopped and looked up and down the bench.

Kristin couldn't take it any longer. "Unless what, Mr. Burrows?"

"Unless the Blazers decide to accept this invitation."

"What invitation?" screamed Jeni and Lauren at the same time.

Dad unfolded the paper. "As last year's State champs, the Blazers have been invited to a National Invitational Tournament hosted by the University of Oklahoma. Forty of the best teams in the country have been invited. Including us."

There were wide eyes, open mouths, and an awesome silence.

"So what do you think, Blazers? We've got three weeks. Can we get ready to face some of the best teams in the country?"

Of course we could!